The Ghost of You

Heather Graham

Prologue

Reno, Nevada
1869

Micah Stratford rode hard, pushing his fine chestnut to a lathered sweat. In a far corner of his mind, he knew he was all but killing an animal that had served him faithfully and well. But the heinous bastard Waverly Adams had Eliza, and Micah would readily die himself before he let the man hurt her in any way.

He had a chance. Bo Harding, Micah's ranch hand, had told Micah with his dying breath that it had been Waverly Adams who had gunned him down, and taken Eliza, furious that he'd found no sign of a silver claim when he'd come to the house.

Waverly! Waverly's the kind of man who had gone to war when the nation had torn apart—only to find just how much he loved killing. The man had said, in a group of his pawing, mauling, sycophant that there was nothing like it, nothing like seeing the light go out in a man's eye, his body shake in a hanging, his blood run hot and sweet and then cold.

Oak Feed Saloon stretched just ahead of him on the spit of road that housed the heart of the Reno, officially a town just back a year in 1868. The bank, the dry goods store, Henry Dean's Law Offices, and a few other cluttered businesses.

Micah headed straight for the saloon. Leaving his poor old Derby in the street, he burst through the swinging doors.

Waverly Adams was there, just as he'd expected, playing poker, his cards—with three aces in the hand—on the table before him. He was playing with Matt Dowel and Blood-Bath Boyd, and they all seemed to be expecting him, grinning as Micah burst in.

More of Waveryly's henchmen were at the bar. Old Sweeney was playing at the piano, and Darla Green was on the little stage, singing her heart out for bastards who didn't give a whit. While she sang like a canary, she made her money naked on a bed with the filthy vermin who frequented the place.

The doors kept swinging; Old Sweeney stopped playing and scurried away. Darla stopping singing, froze, and then ran from the stage.

"I want Eliza," Micah told Waverly flatly. "I want her back now, and if you've injured so much as a hair on her head, Waverly, I'll..."

"You'll what?" Waverly didn't even rise. He just grinned and waved a hand in the air, motioning around him. "These fellows used to be your friend, Micah, just like you used to be my friend. But, then you turned all squeamish, like an old woman. Couldn't do what needed to be done." He leaned forward, suddenly, his smile gone, his face taut with anger. "And now, now that we've lost the war—because of yellow-bellied cowards like you—you want to hold out on your friends."

"I never cottoned to killing women, children, boys, and old men, you sick bastard," Micah told him. "I didn't want to murder civilians—and I never did nothing against you, I just took myself out of the gang, and I went and lived my own life. I want my wife back."

"I want the claim deed to that silver mine on your property," Waverly said.

"There is no claim deed on my property!" Micah said, "I don't know who told you there was, but there isn't one. I'm a rancher, trying to get a herd together, trying to grow some food—trying to survive in this world of ours. Give me my wife back!"

"Well, there she is, son, there she is!"

Waverly directed him to look up to the balcony, and there she was, being held by another of Waverly's men—Dead-eye Dick, as he had come to be called.

"Simon, get away from her," Micah said quietly. Eliza was looking down at him, her long golden hair a tangle around her face, her eyes pleading with him, even at a distance. Beautiful. His wife, so very, very beautiful, and good...loving.

The war years had been true hell; he'd been with Waverly first as militia, and in those days Waverly had just killed. Killed and killed. The day that they'd attacked the farmhouse on the prairie and gunned down everyone there, Micah had walked away. He hadn't deserted; he hadn't wanted to be shot up by either side, he'd gotten himself assigned to a cavalry unit as a sharp-shooter.

That's where he'd met Eliza, the daughter of his captain.

Miraculously, she had fallen in love with him. Her father had been killed in the fighting, and when it had all been over, they had left the east behind, determined to make a new life.

And they had done so...

Until Waverly had shown up out here, killing those who wouldn't sell to him, grabbing up land, looking for silver. And now...

Eliza was staring down at him, pleading with her eyes. He could almost hear the silken beauty of her voice.

Please...whatever they do to me...doesn't matter. We'll get through this...

Back away—he should back away. But, he was carrying a hand-crafted repeating revolver, and he had seven shots, six in the chamber, one in the barrel.

I'll talk to the man, I'll tell him anything, tell him he can take whatever piece of my property he wants...

But Simon hadn't been known as *Dead-eye Dick* for nothing. He had Eliza. He held her with his right hand, and with his left, he held his infamous Colt, waving it dangerously close to her head.

He could kill her, he could kill her...

He saw Simon's eyes, and knew—Simon and the others didn't want to kill Eliza. They wanted to torture her, cut her...have her, and then, probably, kill her.

There was no choice. He drew his modified revolver.

"I'm so sorry, my love, time to get the bad guys," he said softly, and then, "*Run, Eliza, run!*"

He began to fire.

Simon fell dead in a flash, and then Waverly, and then...

Bullets flew everywhere.

He brought down five of the bastards, and then, of course, he'd known that a bullet would find him, knew that he was going to die.

And he was lucky; he was struck straight in the heart, and he fell, and on his lips was a prayer as he did so...

"I will find you, my sweet Eliza, in this life...or the next."

Chapter 1

"Thank you!" Sienna Johnston told the clerk at the coffee pick-up counter. The clerk smiled at her. He was a nice guy, a man in his mid-forties she thought, balding slightly, but with a slightly chubby, baby face. His name, according to the pin on his shirt, was Ernie. She'd seen him deal patiently with a nasty woman who obviously hadn't slept in days and fix an order for a confused older man. She smiled back at him, and then realized suddenly that—even though she'd intended to be very nice herself to make up for the people before her—she was looking past him. One of the managers at the casino—tall, slim, and svelte, dressed handsomely in a suit—was nearby talking with another man.

And it was that other man who had caught her attention.

What he was wearing wasn't exactly an old-fashioned railway frock or duster; it had a far more modern cut. And his hat wasn't exactly old west, but, it was wide-brimmed, and certainly meant to hold back the Nevada sun. It wasn't just his apparel that so garnered her attention though—it was his face, no, really it was everything about him. He was tall, appeared to be well built—not overly-muscled, but broad-shouldered, fit—wiry, perhaps—and lithe. He moved with tremendous ease, the tail of the coat following him. His hair was long, just hitting his shoulders in light brown, reckless waves. He had intense gray eyes, large, and set in a face with good cheekbones and a rugged chin.

As an artist, she noticed every single detail and she wished she could ask him to stand still for a few minutes; she would love to sketch him.

It was rude to stare, of course, so she fought the urge to do so; she took the two cups of coffee over to the table where Lucy Calder was sitting waiting for her.

"I want to gamble, and...I want to gamble!" Lucy said, smiling her thanks as she accepted her coffee. "Okay, so, I'm not rich enough to gamble, gamble, but, I'm so excited to be away, to be here! Oh, that sounds terrible—I adore Conner and Morgan, but, I..."

Lucy let out a little sigh, her head bobbing, and her red curls dancing around her face. She had a gamine, heart-shaped face, and the ability to spend most of her day smiling.

Sienna grinned at her friend. "It's okay—you're a great wife and mom. Everyone needs a break!"

Lucy was also an artist, now concentrating her efforts on book covers—she loved books, and to her, it was the most wonderful thing in the world to create art that induced someone to pick up a good book. She and Sienna had been friends since childhood, going to all the same schools—even choosing the same art school--they were both silent types, who liked to be alone when they worked. Sometimes though, when they were home, they'd go sketch on Jackson Square together. Lucy had concentrated on graphics, while Sienna had concentrated on her visual arts, sketching, portraits, and painting. Still, it was most often a solitary endeavor in which their concentration was on their work, so they were both excited to have taken this trip together.

For Sienna it was business—though, of course, fun as well. It had been her idea to come to the conference they were attending. They were looking to network, to meet people, and, in her case, to do some approved sketches, and take quick video interviews as well. She was about to open a restaurant called "Book Your Table" on Magazine Street in their home city of New Orleans. While they would have the opportunity to mingle with many of the authors for whom Lucy had done covers, Sienna had scheduled appointments with a number of those authors as well—doing little videos of them that would play in her themed restaurant rooms. Sienna had done original art work for a few covers Lucy had designed, simply because she loved books so much, but the true love of her craft came when she was sketching and painting what she saw that intrigued her—and the man in the duster intrigued her.

She loved her art—and books—but, she was really here for her sketches and videos.

Book Your Table had long been a dream for Sienna, but, coming from a city known for its cuisine, she had to be careful that it was done right and that her vision was implemented in the most unique manner possible. She had wonderful chefs lined up, and she just needed to finish her dream décor before their grand opening, planned in a month.

There would be seven dedicated rooms and a play room—the play room, naturally, would be filled with children's books, soft comfy chairs, little trampolines, and more. Then there would be the genre rooms, and those would be sci-fi and fantasy, horror, mystery and thriller, history, young adult, non-fiction, and, of course, romance. Customers would be encouraged to bring books they had finished and wanted to pass on, and everyone would be encouraged to take a book when they left. Some new books would be sold in the bookshop, and, of course, since it would be her shop, she'd get to be the buyer!

The author videos she planned on filming on this trip— showing in each themed room at the touch of a button—would be an extra special touch. She was excited to begin.

But, they were a day early. Here now for nothing but fun. No classes, panels, or other related business functions started until tomorrow—including her interviews. Lucy wanted to gamble and they both wanted to sight-see.

They sat in the hotel's small coffee shop on the ground floor. Buzzers and bells sounded from everywhere—just about all of the lower level of the Reno Western Grand was taken up with slot machines, poker tables, and every conceivable form of casino play known to man.

The very intriguing man she had noted was taking his leave, heading toward the elevators with the other man who was wearing the very proper suit. Sienna inclined her head, indicating his direction. "Don't stare, but, boy, I...I would love to sketch him!"

Lucy turned, her assessment obvious—had the man been looking.

"I said not to stare!" Sienna said with a sigh.

"Sorry! Couldn't help it—very interesting. Not just good-looking...rough, rugged, very macho looking—but, with a great smile. What a super subject—you're right. I wonder if his personality is as cool as his looks? Oh, well, I'll bet he's married. All the good ones are married."

"Lucy, you're married," Sienna reminded her friend. Lucy was married to a great guy, Conner, and the two were very happy together. But, they also had a toddling boy, Morgan—two-and-a-half-years old--and these five days on her own was a break for Lucy, endorsed by the man who loved her so much.

"I know, and I'm a happy camper. I'm looking for you."

"Don't, please...don't."

"You broke it off with Cliff a long time ago now," Sienna reminded her.

"And, I'm fine. I'm busy—I'm opening a restaurant, remember?"

Lucy shrugged and looked at Sienna again. "Okay, I just think it would be cool if you stumbled upon tall, dark—or light—and handsome, but I'll behave. My coffee and I are going to a slot machine. I see one with witches over there calling to me." After a few steps toward the slot machine in question, Lucy turned back, "You're too picky—you need to date once in a while."

"Hey!"

"Okay, I'll quit trying to make you happy."

"I'm just busy, in real life, and now...time to gamble—we'll find some penny slot machines without a million lines so that a penny slot doesn't turn into five bucks a spin. But, I want to see some sights, too, okay? We can gamble, and if you're winning...well, I still want to get to Virginia City. And I want to go to that cool little museum we saw in the book last night. So, if you want to keep gambling, it's fine with me—seriously—but, I'll head out alone after lunch," Sienna said.

"Fine, but, I think there's a cool little ghost machine, right by the witch machine."

Sienna followed Lucy, sat down at the machine and put her money in. She had to admit, the graphics were pretty amazing. But, the first time a "wild" square jumped up and filled the screen, she startled, sitting back.

The ghost of a cowboy on the screen seemed to see her just as she saw him; he grinned, and then, he filled the center line on the screen, laughed—and winked at her.

"Time to take down the bad guys!" the cowboy announced.

The smile was amazing; the graphics and animation were excellent as the smiling cowboy turned to bone and dust, and the screen filled a sign that said she was a winner.

It seemed a little odd—being a winner, with the cowboy decomposing before her, but...

Anyway, she wasn't enough of a winner to make up for what she lost. But, the game was fun, still she couldn't get over the fact that the cowboy seemed to be watching her and smiling at her.

They didn't have to wait until after lunch—Lucy lost what she'd allowed herself to lose within an hour.

***

"Something is going on," Milt Conway said, shaking his head. "I know that the hotel isn't considered liable in anyway, but, I'm sure something was going on. I feel something started here—I have to know if I'm right. I can't pinpoint it, but, I have to know what happened."

Micah Stratford looked at him, not discounting his words, but equally aware that the police had been to the casino, and that they had nothing—the woman in question had been seen checking out of the hotel and leaving.

Catherine Maddox—a young woman who had now been missing forty-eight hours and had been officially reported as missing by her sister—had last been seen by a reliable witness in a local pharmacy, where she had chatted with the clerk and said that she'd been thinking about a day in Virginia City before heading home.

"And," Milt continued, "if something is going on, I have to stop it—whether the police believe that she's just gone on holiday or not. I have several thousand writers coming in today and tomorrow—I have to know what it is, come on, Micah, I'm desperate."

Micah Stratford had just spent the last few hours at the casino; he'd gone over the video surveillance tapes with security. He hadn't seen anything outside the usual. Someone thrilled because he or she had hit a jackpot, and someone else with a look of hangdog defeat—completely out of money. He'd stopped to talk to Gary Morgan—tall, dignified, designer-suited—and one of the morning managers on the floor, a man who watched over the machines, the tables, and the twenty-four-hour café. Ernie Anderson, at the cash register in the coffee shop, had told him that he'd seen Catherine every morning, and that she'd been sweet and polite, always.

Gary had been at a loss—he, too, had seen Catherine Maddox. He hadn't seen anyone bothering her or following her.

There was plenty of video, of course—it was a casino. So, painstakingly going through the time that she'd been there, Micah had seen many images of Catherine Maddox. Playing at the machines, laughing at the café, riding the elevator, up and down. At no point had anyone accompanied her to her room. At no point had it appeared that anyone had been bothering her or coercing her to do anything or go anywhere.

He knew, of course, why Milt Conway, a security manager at the casino, was so concerned; it was the young woman who had disappeared from a nearby casino and been found dead a year after her disappearance.

Micah remembered it all too clearly.

The memory was painful and strange.

No one had even known her real name—she had been a 'working girl,' and the friend who reported her missing wasn't even sure that she'd gone missing. All she had known was that she the girl had gone by Lady Blue, and that she had expected to see her at the casino again.

But, she had gone missing, and, because of what she did for a living and the fact that no one seemed to know her real name, no one ever gave a great deal of attention to the case. If there was even a case at all.

Until she was found.

While not a cop—not here, not now, in Reno--Micah had been instrumental in finding her. He'd been out with a friend, Artie Flannigan—who was a Reno detective—when terrified hikers had called about finding a human bone beneath a tree when they'd stopped to rest.

The bone they'd found turned out to belong to mountain lion, but while answering the call, they'd discovered an odd mound near the site and he'd been determined to investigate. Artie had agreed.

That's how the body of the missing woman had been discovered in a pine box. The police believed that she'd been held captive somewhere for several days before she'd been buried.

Buried in a simple pine box. Buried alive.

That was what the medical examiner had told them.

The body, still unidentified, had never been claimed. Her friend, another 'working girl,' had long since left Las Vegas. When she'd been discovered, her condition had touched police and all those who had seen her, guilt had set in, and no matter what she had done for a living, they continued to refer to her as, "Lady Blue."

Another woman having disappeared—even if it was for only forty-eight hours at the moment—was a serious concern.

Catherine Maddox's sister had reported her missing two days ago; the police had immediately done everything humanly possible to follow her trail. However, while the casinos had cameras everywhere, not all streets, pharmacies, restaurants, or other facilities did.

"I won't give up," Micah promised.

"I know you won't, and the cops...they all respect you," Milt said.

That was true, and it was a boon. Micah knew it. He hadn't been a cop for a few years now; and when he had been, it had been back in Chicago. During a bizarre and deadly bank heist, he had managed to take down one of the robbers and free the twenty hostages, something for which he was grateful. But, no matter how well that had gone, he couldn't forget the young couple he hadn't managed to save—shot while negotiators were trying to talk to the robbers, before he'd made it through the back to take down the man holding the rest of the hostages.

Then, his life had changed. His fault. He'd watched beautiful young people gunned down, and he hadn't been able to stop it.

He'd spent months with the police shrinks, his father had remarried and wanted to move to Hawaii with his new bride, the old homestead needed someone, and he didn't want to remain in Chicago anymore. He was happy for his father—who had adored his mother and mourned her death for well over a decade before contemplating a date, much less marriage.

Micah's own relationship of several years had fallen apart—his fault, he'd been acting like a zombie—and a change of venue seemed like a good thing, the right move.

So, he'd come home. He'd done his best to whip their small, family museum and restaurant into shape, and he'd tried to spend time with old friends, moving on.

Artie had wanted him to apply for the force in Reno; he'd told Artie—and himself—that he was too busy keeping the museum and restaurant going. But, he spent time with Artie, and talked with him about his cases—especially the case in which he'd been so involved, that of Lady Blue. He had also helped Milt pull a sting when he'd suspected a guest was helping himself to women's purses when they'd just struck a nice jackpot. But, the thief had never offered anyone the least harm—he had, in fact, been a nice fellow, and Micah was glad that he hadn't been the cop who had to take him in, or prosecutor who was going to have to put him away.

"Don't give up, please. I have a bad feeling about this," Milt said.

Reno had good cops and the casino dozens of men working security...

But, Milt was his friend, way back, like Artie, he'd been in the same school and on the same teams as Micah. Milt knew that although he wasn't on a payroll, he could trust Micah and that Micah was good at seeking out the details that might matter.

"I went through the videos; I walked the casino, which, of course, I'll do again," Micah said. "I look at every face..."

He paused. He did look at faces. And, he found himself remembering one in particular. Pretty girl, long, dark-blond hair, tall, lithe in her movements, with a great face, high cheekbones, generous mouth, beautiful eyes. He remembered the way she smiled as she thanked the cashier at the café. Writer? Writers were filing in to the hotel. Somehow, she managed to be cute, casual—and, also a bit sensual and elegant. He'd noted her—and her friend. And now, he was thinking about her.

He should be thinking about a kidnapper.

But, for a moment, his mind was taken by memories of that smile...and the way both she and her friend had looked at him when he was leaving. He lowered his head—obviously, they didn't think that he had seen them look. He had.

Maybe he would see her again.

That thought spurred something within him.

He hoped that Catherine Maddox had simply gone off on a trip and forgotten to tell anyone that she'd had the sudden urge to go on to Las Vegas.

He didn't think, though, that was going to prove to be the case. There was a kidnapper and murderer out here somewhere, and he'd lain dormant, or taken women never reported missing, and hidden them so well that they were still lost to law enforcement?

But, now—if he was right, and the man who had killed Lady Blue had gone for Catherine Maddox—he might have chosen the wrong victim, one who had a loving sister. While the first victim hadn't even been recognized as missing for months, the information regarding Catherine Maddox's disappearance was being blasted on the news.

What if this spurred the killer into going on a binge?

What if he went after more young women, like the pretty blond and her friend?

He had no idea why he was jumping to such conclusions— Catherine Maddox could have simply forgotten to call her sister and gone off for a spa weekend. Even she had been kidnapped, Catherine hadn't necessarily been taken by the same people.

But, there was something. Instinct, maybe. He believed that the woman had been taken, and, he believed that it just might be the same person who had buried a woman in a pine box off the side of a hiking trail.

"I've got some good friends who will give me access to *VICAP* records; I'm going to see what I can find here. I'll go back through the video after," Micah promised Milt. And then he told him, determined, "I will find out what happened."

He would.

He had to.

He envisioned the next victim being the young woman he had seen that morning, buried deep in the earth, gasping desperately for her last breaths.

Crazy.

He would most probably never see her again.

But...

Something in him, like a strange whisper in his mind, suggested that he would.

He needed to get back to his own computer—and to make some connections with old friends who would be happy to help on   a   case   like   this.

Chapter 2

"Where to first?" Lucy asked.

Her head in the guidebook, Sienna answered quickly. "The little museum—it's only open until five, other attractions in Virginia City are opened later."

They were out in front of the casino, ready to head out.

Sienna keyed the address into her car service app, and they waited in front of the hotel, watching neon signs blink and shine as they did so. Reno wasn't Las Vegas—the latter had taken over as the mecca of gaming, but it was impressive with its hotels and restaurants, and, perhaps, lovelier in its landscape—they were at the foot of the mountains, near Lake Tahoe, and the scenery could be breathtaking.

When they arrived at the museum, a billboard noted that it was "The Stratford Ranch and Museum, featuring My Kitchen, open for breakfast, lunch, and fine dining."

"Hey, maybe we should have come here second," Sienna noted, reading the sign about the dining. "I wonder just how 'fine' it is? And what they serve, of course." She looked around; they were right on the path that seemed to lead to an old barn. Paddocks surrounded it, and while Sienna didn't see cattle, sheep, or chickens, there were five horses—beautiful ones—kicking up their heels and running about in one of the paddocks.

"There's an old house back there—looks like an old ranch house," Lucy said, pointing to the far right of the barn as they walked up to it.

As they reached a side door that announced "Entry," Sienna felt someone come up behind them. More tourists; she'd seen people parking in the lot when they'd arrived and several walking around the property, many admiring the horses.

At the door, Lucy made a face. "Bet the old geezer who runs this place lives there," she said.

"I'll bet he does," a deep, rich voice announced behind them.

They turned to see the man who had spoken was the same man who had intrigued Sienna at the casino.

Both women were awkwardly silent for a moment, staring. "Maybe," Sienna said, getting herself together. She smiled, "We saw you earlier, right?"

He nodded. "Coffee. Yes. I'm Micah Stratford. I have a few 'ins' here. If I'm not being too forward, come with me—we'll skip the reception desk."

He walked ahead. Sienna hesitated; Lucy gave her a glare and followed him, and Sienna did so quickly, too. The young woman at the ticket counter just inside the barn door smiled and waved at the man—Micah Stratford—and they followed him in. Once past the desk, he stopped. "I'll leave you here, and hope you enjoy the place," he said, offering them each a handshake.

His handshake was warm; his eyes, touching on Sienna as he smiled, were a fascinating gray.

"Thank you," she told him, and added, "I'm Sienna Johnston and this is Lucy Calder. Thank you, Micah."

"It was nothing; I love this place. I hope you do, too."

He left them, and, turning, headed back out to the entry.

"Nice!" Lucy said.

"It was very nice of him to get us in."

"I mean 'nice' as in him!" Lucy said. "So...which way?"

The barn had been partitioned off with false, moveable walls, but, right by the entry, there were arrows pointing to the left and the right. To the left, they could find, Settlers Arrive, The Founding of Reno, Now in the City, and, to the right appeared to be, Myths and Legends, and, Bizarre Stories.

"Bizarre stories!" Lucy said.

"Yes, but, bizarre stories are better when you know about the bizarre area where they were taking place," Sienna said.

"Okay, you go left and I'll go right, we'll switch in the middle, and see what worked!"

Sienna went left.

She quickly fell in love with the layout of the museum. Plaques gave dates and facts while copies of old photographs, greatly enlarged, showed what was happening where, and when. Old saddles and mining tools were displayed, giving a sense of personality and reality to all that was told. By the 1850s, a few setters had arrived, but it had been in 1859 that Charles William Fuller had come and settled a piece of land on the Truckee River, and opened a small hotel. He also built a bridge, allowing for travelers from both sides of the river. The river provided for a fertile valley in the high desert area that sat at the foot of the Sierra Nevada. It was off the California Trail, and allowed a respite for those heading west. But, while some came to settle and farm or ranch, many had come because gold had been discovered in the Virginia City area in 1850, and in 1859, a silver load had been discovered.

Fuller sold his property to Charles Lake, and Lake added a mill, a kiln, stables, and more—and renamed the hotel Lake's Crossing.

Lake also made a deal with the Central Pacific Railroad, and—in exchange for the land Lake had given the railroad—a depot came into existence. A railroad official named the community *Reno,* after Union Major General Jesse Lee Reno—killed during the Civil War.

The community officially became the town of Reno in 1868, and, since the Civil War had ended in 1865, many men, bereft of land, loved ones, or, simply needing to escape the devastation of the east, traveled west. Reno was on its way—but, not without conflict. Bar fights abounded; the war had ended, but, not the old hatreds. Good men tried to put them aside, but there would always be those still fighting.

Sienna continued reading her way around the room, but, a break in the false walls caught her attention.

There was a picture on the wall in the myth and legend area of the museum. Drawn to it, she made her way through the partition.

She stared at the old, enlarged photograph. It was that of a handsome, rugged-looking cowboy. She frowned, studying it.

It's the same cowboy who winked at me in the graphics of the slot machine!

A chill touched her, and she tried to shake it off. Maybe, whoever had designed the slot machine, had been to the museum. That was it; that had to be it.

"Eliza!" someone said softly behind her.

She turned to tell whoever it was that they were mistaken—she wasn't Eliza.

But, her mouth froze, wide open.

She was staring at the cowboy, the man from the slot machine—a mirror image of the man in the old, blown-up photograph.

"Eliza!" he said again, his whisper heart-breaking in the tone. And then, just as he had said in the slot machine, he said, "Time to catch the bad guys!"

She tried to make her mouth work; she wanted to say that she wasn't Eliza, and, at the same time...

She wondered what it would have been like to have been Eliza, and to have been loved as much as this man had obviously loved Eliza, so apparent in the tone of his voice, in his eyes, in the way he looked at her.

"Hey!"

Startled, Sienna turned away from the man. Lucy was coming toward her, smiling broadly.

"I love, love, love this place!" Lucy said. "Coolest legends, one about a miner who was killed and is still supposed to caress women's necks when they're wearing silver, and another..."

Her voice trailed as she looked at Sienna. "What's the matter?"

The man, the cowboy, was gone. Almost as if he had vanished into thin air.

"This—this man in the picture; I just saw him," Sienna said.

"Ah, see, I told you—myths and legends first!" Lucy said. "If you'd come with me, you'd know that he was the man who built this place, and that he died, taking out six outlaws who had kidnapped his wife and were running this area of the town. I'll bet the owner hires the dude to walk around and give people a taste of the old days. Oh, and guess what?" she asked.

Sienna didn't have to answer. Micah was back, smiling as he walked up to the two of them.

"My namesake," he said. "Grandfather—many times over. He killed the bad guys and went down himself, but his wife, Eliza, went on to farm and ranch the property—free to do so with the criminal element wiped out—and, of course, mourning her husband to the end of her days. Oh, yes, and the old geezer who owns the place does live here, at the ranch house," he told them.

Sienna might have resented being made to look like a fool, but she was captivated by his smile, and the fact that he obviously had intended that they really enjoy the museum.

However, she did feel that she needed to mention that he'd been a jerk.

"Nice, you played us. So, you also hire someone who looks just like him to wander around, right?" she asked, a little edge in her voice.

He frowned. "I didn't mean to play you—I just thought that you really wanted to enjoy the place, and...anyway. There are no actors here. You saw Chris Sweeney at the entrance, and there is a man—Justin Powell—who maintains the exhibits and watches out for any vandalism—of course, we have cameras, too—but...Justin is sixty. Long white beard—doesn't look a thing like the original Micah."

"Well, then, someone is fooling around in your museum," Sienna said.

He frowned. "Not sanctioned by me. I promise you, I will check the video feed, and I will find out what's going on." He shrugged. "I hope you enjoyed the museum," he said. "I wish you'd come later, though. The café is fun for breakfast and lunch, but Chef Mitchell comes in most nights to run the kitchens, and he is legendary, out of New Orleans—"

"Chef Mitchell!" Sienna said. "I knew he'd left New Orleans, but, I'd thought he was going to San Francisco."

"We're from New Orleans," Lucy said. "And Sienna is opening a restaurant."

"Well, then, you must come back," Micah said, "on me, please."

"Thank you," Sienna said. "That's really kind of you, but—"

"No strings attached," he assured her. "Just let me know when you want to come."

"Tonight," Lucy said. "Tonight would be great."

"Lucy, we don't want to take advantage," Sienna murmured.

And, yet, really, she did! She was a little bit angry, but, also fascinated. She couldn't remember the last time she had felt such an attraction. And yet, she sensed what a mistake it might be. He could be married, and she'd just be torturing herself. He could have a girlfriend, or a partner, or...

"Hey, we're coming!" Lucy said. And she grinned. "I'm here on a bit of a budget—husband is watching the toddler while I'm out of town—and I have to admit, I'd adore a fine meal created by Chef Mitchell—on you!"

Sienna winced.

But, Micah Stratford laughed.

"Please, I'll have a table waiting for you, say, any time after six."

"We'll be back!" Lucy promised.

Micah inclined his head slightly. "See you then." He started to walk away, but, turned back. "If you want to see Micah, he's buried up at Terrace Hill, Virginia City. The cemetery is old and fascinating—I think you'd enjoy it."

***

The more he saw her, the more Micah wanted to know her—watch over her, perhaps. It was ridiculous to think, of course, that with all the people in Reno—a large portion of them being attractive young women—Sienna Johnston might be the next victim.

Libido taking over logic?

He met attractive women all the time. His friends were attractive women. He'd seen a ton of attractive women, but...

There was something about her.

He gritted his teeth, aggravated with himself.

At the moment, he needed to concentrate. They needed to find Catherine Maddox quickly—them finding her quickly might be her only chance at living.

He sat at his desk in the ranch house, going back over the police reports, and searching through VICAP as he did so.

The medical examiner had estimated that the first victim, Lady Blue, had been kept prisoner for several days before being buried alive; chaffing at her wrists and ankles indicated that she had fought rope bonds for at least eighty-eighty hours before her death. Mercifully, that had come quickly, or so the medical examiner had believed, taking in factors such as available oxygen, and the heat that might have arisen in such a box beneath the earth.

Catherine Maddox had been at the casino-hotel for a week before checking out. That led Micah to believe that Milt had been right—she'd been stalked while there. Her assailant had noted her comings and goings, and maybe even befriended her.

He had to see the videos again.

He glanced at his watch; he was going to head back to the security room at the casino; there had to be something on video. Something they were all missing.

His guests weren't due back for several hours. Of course, his staff at the restaurant would take care of them, but...

He'd be seeing to it himself that they had dinner—and were taken home after. He could spend the entire night looking at video footage, over, and then over again, if need be.

Chapter 3

Sienna quickly fell in love with Virginia City. Board sidewalks and restored buildings—many of them casinos, tempting Lucy—gave way to wonderful museums that gave the history of the western town a sense of still being with them.

Sienna wanted to see everything.

Lucy told her she was just like a Chevy Chase character in a movie she had just seen on Netflix, one in which he'd run through every museum in Paris and beyond in five minutes.

"It's just so...I love it!"

Though not far from Reno, the history was similar. Henry Comstock, and the "Comstock Load," had brought out settlers, and for a time, the town had boomed. They enjoyed just walking the streets, getting the feel—and, as Lucy had said—running through museums. They knew if they wanted to see the cemetery by light, they had to move.

"Wow!" Lucy breathed. "Okay, you can rush me. This is all incredible."

Silver Hill Cemetery and Golden Hill Cemetery were set on terraces, making a beautiful, windswept climb up the terrain.

Lucy was immediately running around, fascinated. "You can tell who was rich, and who was poor—oh, and read the stones and the markers—everyone seems to have come from somewhere else. And, I love the way that they're all...well, these iron fences, and the stonework! And the grave markers are in stone, and some are marble...and some, you can read. And, some you can't!"

"I guess some people still have relatives in the area, who keep up the graves," Sienna said.

She stood still. A slightly chilly breeze had crept into being as they wandered the terraces.

She shouldn't feel chilled—there were many people wandering the terraces of the cemeteries. In fact, she felt guilty—they hadn't opted to take a tour, but they could clearly hear a young guide who was speaking loudly so as to be heard by her entire group.

She was telling them that years before, the cemetery had been even more beautiful—though perhaps, it was more haunting now. But, time and weather were taking their toll, along with soil erosion and, in some cases, vandalism. She pointed out different sections of the cemetery, talked about groups, such as the Masons, Virginia City firefighters, and more, and, of course, the different sections for various religious groups. She pointed out an area that was down to a small stone fence, broken wooden crosses, and a bit of scrub grass. "Wooden crosses and markers didn't always survive!" she noted, and then, she pointed down the terrace.

"And there, of course, just down the next 'step' on the terrace, fenced in by that beautiful ironwork, is the Stratford grave. Eliza Stratford, who survived the shoot-out that killed her husband, didn't have the kind of money needed for such a grave—the funds were donated by a grateful community to bury Micah Stratford, desperate to save his beloved Eliza, he'd managed to save them all. They'd provided the funds for the stone, and for the angel, and, of course, after, more of the Stratford family were buried there, including Eliza, who is, of course, buried at his side."

"Oh, we just have to go see that!" Lucy said. "Free dinner!" she called over her shoulder.

Lucy hurried off, and Sienna followed her.

A handsome iron gate surrounded the graves. An angel had been sculpted to stand over them. "Well, twenty years later, but, they rest together," Lucy said. "Oh, look, over there—a group of graves for children. That's always so sad. At least we can prevent many more deaths from terrible fevers now, huh?"

Lucy had started moving again; Sienna felt frozen, and, at first, she wasn't sure why. She was staring at the stone that denoted Micah's birth and death dates. He had died young, and his life must have been brutal. He'd been just twenty at the start of the war; just twenty-nine when he had died.

Leaning over the iron gate, Sienna read the inscription on Eliza's tomb. She had most likely written the words herself, before her death. "My life now gone, I lie here at last, the years as nothing now. For a thousand lifetimes I'd have waited, longing for the past. One day again, we shall meet, sacred to love, and far above."

"Eliza!"

Sienna heard the whisper and turned.

He was there again; the man from the slot machine, from the museum...from the portrait!

He was there, his eyes in torment, his arm outstretched...

"Time to get the bad guys, oh, Eliza..."

He turned and walked away, toward the tour group, and beyond them. The dying sun cast down a wicked ray of sun.

Sienna lifted a hand to shield her eyes, suddenly determined to go after him.

She started to run in his direction, dodging fenced plots and random headstones, but, just beyond the group, the sun shifted again blinding her for a minute. When she could see again, she thought that she saw him, nothing more than a shadow against the dying day.

And then, he was gone.

***

Micah studied the matches he was drawing up in the VICAP system—not perfect matches, but, close enough to make Micah think that there was a killer who had been quietly prowling for his victims and disposing of them—after holding them for a few days, torturing them perhaps, and then...

A young woman had been found dead in a frozen lake in northern Oregon, another, on the border with California. Yet another had been found in the southeast corner of Washington State—beneath road work that had just been completed and covered over. Each had been a woman between twenty and thirty years of age. The first three had been prostitutes, and since none of the bodies had been disposed of in the same way, the possibility of a connection might have been remote. Two had been junkies, and the third had been well on her way to liver failure.

He wondered if anyone else would make the connection to the disappearance of Catherine Maddox—or Lady Blue, with these other women.

What connected them was the chaffing marks, found at their wrists and ankles.

Of course, there was another problem; there were no exact dates to trace. The way the bodies had been found, the medical examiners had only been able to estimate very approximate times of death.

If the killer had taken Catherine Maddox, a woman with a family, a teacher by trade, he was upping his game, or growing cocky—someone would definitely be looking for her, long before her body might finally be discovered in another such dump site.

He had to see the videos from the casino again and watch for anything—anything at all.

He glanced at his watch; he still had a great deal of the afternoon left, and...

Even if he was intrigued and anxious to see Sienna and Lucy again, this was critical.

If he was right, there was a kidnapper and a killer at work, and he was growing bolder. Catherine Maddox just might be alive, if they could get to her quickly enough.

And...

Any young women in the area might be in danger.

Any young women...

Including Sienna or Lucy.

***

Sienna sat in the restaurant at the Stratford museum, trying to enjoy herself, and trying to be happy that Lucy was having such a wonderful time.

She just couldn't stop thinking about the cowboy who kept appearing before her.

Or the fact that the man looked exactly like the man in the picture. She kept trying to figure out if Micah resembled the man, and, he might, in a way, but far from exact.

Okay, so, a slot machine developer or creator had seen the picture of the Micah Stratford who had lived long ago--and died, cleaning up his little section of Reno. That would explain the resemblance in the slot machine.

Her seeing the man—in the flesh—was not so easy to explain. Unless the current Micah Stratford was using her and Lucy. Maybe she was supposed to start saying that a ghost was running around—the ghost of slot-machine game—torturing her. Oh, yeah, and he happened to have been an antecedent to a man who owned a museum all about the past. What better way to encourage more tourism?

That had to be it; Micah Stratford had hired an actor to run around looking like his ancestor!

He hadn't been there when they'd arrived, but the restaurant host, a young man in a western apparel, had known who they were, and had expected them. They were seated at a table by the huge hearth that dominated the room.

A nice table.

And their waitress had informed them that they were welcome to anything on the menu, and that Mr. Stratford was delighted that they'd come.

"Because we know writers!" Lucy said, delighted to be sipping a white wine recommended specially to go with the lobster-infused fish they had ordered. "He's being this nice because he knows we're in town for a writers' conference. He wants us to get people out here, and we'll all write him up with great reviews on travel sites! Which is fine—I can gamble a little more with the money I've saved on dinner tonight!"

Sienna winced. "Lucy, I think we're being used, and not because we're at a writer's conference. I keep seeing that actor he hired!"

"You said that you saw him in the cemetery—I didn't! And I didn't see him in the museum. You're suffering from some kind of jetlag, and we didn't even come from that far!"

"Lucy, he's in a slot machine—the same guy who has his picture hanging on the wall. Okay, I got that. But he was here, in the museum, and he was at the cemetery. Stratford hired him."

She'd been so impassioned in her speech that she didn't hear anyone approaching until she heard Micah Stratford ask politely, "May I?" and pull out a chair to join them.

"Thank you!" Lucy told him immediately. "The appetizer is delicious, the cornbread is out of this world, and the menu—so eclectic! Western, Mexican, Cajun, and all-American!"

"Thank you, and I'm so glad you're enjoying the restaurant," Micah said. He crossed one leg over the other, his hands folded before him, and he looked at Sienna, the gray in his eyes as hard as steel. "I have not hired an actor; I have never hired an actor. I've only been running the place a year or so, but, I can also assure you, my father never hired an actor."

She flushed, aware of his anger, and aware again that he was probably the most attractive and compelling man she had met in ages. He was obviously not at all impressed by her, and she was suddenly afraid that she might destroy Lucy's chance of a great dinner. He might be angry enough to see that a check was delivered to them.

No, he wasn't the kind of man who would do that, and she didn't know how she knew it, she just did. The same way she knew she had to stand her ground.

"Mr. Stratford, I'm sorry. It may not be you, but, I swear to you, there is a man running around trying to creep me out or scare me, or...he's in the slot machine. I'm telling you, someone saw the picture of your ancestor, and found an actor who looks just like him."

"Sienna thinks that she saw him at the cemetery," Lucy said. She sighed softly. "I wish I could meet him—the real Micah! I mean, you're a real Micah—didn't mean that you weren't—but, your ancestor must have been something. I read about him, and he knew he would die saving his wife, but he also knew that he had to do it. So romantic! And she raised their children and lived on another twenty years, in love with him all that time!"

"Romantic—and sad," Micah said, "He did take out a really bad element of the population, men who had killed ranchers and anyone who got in their way. But—he did give up his own life. Anyway," he added, "Could you show me this slot machine? I'd love to see it."

Sienna smiled. "It's back at the casino, of course."

He returned her smile, his gray eyes fascinating again. "That's okay—I'm going to drive you all back."

"You don't have to do that, really!" Sienna said. "This dinner was lovely. Really, we can't have you doing more."

"I'd like to see the slot machine," he said, "and, I intend to drive you back anyway." He hesitated. "A woman who had been staying at your hotel disappeared a few days ago. It would make me happy to know that you're back there safely."

"Oh, I saw that on the news this morning!" Lucy said. "Catherine Maddox—that's her name. Her sister has reported her missing." She frowned. "But, the reporter said that she'd checked out of the casino, and I'm assuming that there's security everywhere in the casino."

"In the casino, yes," Micah said.

"We're here for a conference—we'll be surrounded by people all the time," Sienna murmured.

"Which is good," he said. "Writers, tons of them, right?"

"We're actually artists—cover artists. Sienna is incredible, and, if I do say so myself, I'm amazing with graphics, and with the 'E' market these days, it's important that we get into a number of the workshops on marketing and all."

"I'm sure it will be wonderful for you," he said politely.

"Oh, and Sienna is opening a restaurant!" Lucy told him.

For the next thirty minutes, while their food was served, and they ate, Lucy extolled Sienna's virtues, and Sienna winced inwardly, shaking her head when Lucy tried to go on.

They learned that Micah had been in the military out of high school, gone to major in criminal sciences, and been a cop in Chicago until his father had wanted to head to Hawaii, and he'd made the choice to return to Reno.

"And you're not married!" Lucy said.

He shook his head. "Nope, never worked out that way."

"Sienna's not married either!" Lucy offered.

"Lucy!" Sienna protested, compelled to offer Micah and apologetic look.

He just grinned. "When you're ready, I'll get you back."

"Ladies' room?" Lucy asked.

He pointed to the rear of the restaurant; Lucy jumped up to head that way and Sienna excused herself, running after Lucy.

"Lucy! Please, you're throwing me at him!" she said, once they were inside the restroom.

"Am I? Well, it's true—he's not married, you're not married, he's cute as can be and hot as hell, owns his own business...and he likes you, I can tell. You're crazy if you don't at the very least have one wild crazy day with him. Or night!" she added, grinning.

"Lucy, we're here for a conference."

"And, he's nice enough to drive us back to our conference. Because he's worried about some maniac who might grab us up!"

"We don't know him—he could be a maniac ready to grab us up!"

Lucy laughed. "I hardly think he'd leave from his restaurant with us after having us there as invited guests—and then snatch us up. A little obvious to police, huh, don't you think?"

"All right, all right, but, please...some decorum!"

They headed back. Both Sienna and Lucy had worked as waitresses to get through college—he might have bought their dinner for them, but they were going to leave a generous tip for their waitress. Sienna had only herself to worry about, and Lucy was thrilled to be able to use her dinner budget for a few more plays at a slot machine, so Sienna made sure to leave the tip.

"Oh, one more thing—did you ever meet Chef Mitchell?" he asked.

Sienna shook her head.

"He's here, in the kitchen. Come on back, he'll take a break, I'm sure."

"That would be—wonderful," Sienna murmured.

They met Chef Mitchell, and they were delighted to tell him how they'd enjoyed his cuisine in New Orleans, and just how wonderful their food had been that night. He was very nice in return, telling Sienna if she had any questions about her new restaurant, he'd be delighted to help.

When they left, Sienna was compelled to tell Micah thank you; it had meant a great deal to her.

"You're a chef yourself, too?" he asked.

"No, or a bad one, at best. I've just had this idea for a restaurant forever—I managed to find a few chefs I like, enough to cover shifts throughout the week," she told him. "Are you much of a cook?" she asked him.

He grinned. "No. Why do you think I looked for the best I could find."

She smiled. Lucy crawled into the backseat of his Land Rover. She was left to slide in next to Micah.

When they reached the casino, Lucy begged exhaustion and headed up.

That left Sienna alone with Micah.

"Want to show me that machine?" he asked her.

"Of course."

"I swear to you, it's not me—I don't have anyone on payroll or otherwise dressing up as my ancestor. He's kind of a hero around here, and I would never let anyone tarnish his memory."

"Of course not! I didn't mean...I'm sorry."

"No, no, I didn't mean it that way—it's just, well, I don't like it."

"I understand, really."

"No, um, well, we already discussed that a woman who had been staying here went missing, right?"

"Right."

"Makes me suspicious of an unknown character running around in a costume."

"You don't think that...he could be someone...a criminal?"

"I don't know."

Sienna nodded and made her way through the rows of slots, accompanied by the buzzers and bells that sounded continuously. He followed her.

When they reached the machine, a man was at it. Sienna paused. "Sorry," she murmured, but, just as she spoke, the man let out a sigh of aggravation and disgust—and left the machine.

Micah produced a bill and slid it into the machine.

"There's a cowboy square and when it shows up, he covers the screen and says, 'Time to get the bad guys!' He's the bonus," she told Micah.

"Hit the button, let's see what happens."

"We could be here a long time—bonuses don't always pop up," Sienna murmured.

"That's okay, we'll wait. Just play low—he'll come up eventually."

She laughed. "You can hit the buttons."

"No, I'll sit next to you, and you hit them. I'm not much of a gambler—horrible luck at these things. He'll come up for you, maybe."

Sienna laughed. "It's a slot machine—doesn't matter who's pushing the buttons, but..."

She sat; he sat by her. She realized that she liked him there, being close. In truth, she liked him. She just wished that...

He was real. Someone who could be in her life. He was attractive, funny, kind...as long as he wasn't the maniac who might have kidnapped someone!

But, he wasn't. She knew that—though she didn't know how she knew. Maybe she just didn't want him to be. She liked the scent of him, the warmth of him...

"There!" she said.

The cowboy popped onto the screen, only...

It was a different cowboy. A cowboy who didn't resemble Micah's   ancestor   in   any   way,   shape,   or   form.

Chapter 4

After Micah said goodnight to Sienna Johnston, he called Milt. His friend had been in the casino all day.

He was still there.

While Micah waited for him, he thought about Sienna, and the shock on her face when the bonus on the game had popped up.

Then, of course, she had flushed, and looked so disturbed that instead of pointing out the fact that the man portrayed in the graphics wasn't at all the Micah of old, he'd tried to reassure her.

"Maybe someone changed the game during the day," he had told her.

She had looked at him with a frown, as if she wasn't about to accept such a ludicrous idea—they'd know if the game had been changed out, and the casino most likely would not have changed out one slot machine, and not just to change an image in the machine.

"I don't understand!" she said, and he realized just how sincere she had been—and so sure of what she had seen. "I know what I saw, and I saw...a man in this machine who looked just like your ancestor, and, I swear! He was in the museum today, and in the cemetery!"

"Listen, please, you must have seen someone—and there could easily be an actor out there running around as him, though why I swear, I don't know. I need you to believe that it isn't me!"

"I—I do. But, I hope you'll believe me. I'm not crazy, and I'm suffering jetlag, I swear."

"I know," he said, and then added, "I know you're busy—you're here for a convention, but...if you do see this guy again—or, of course, if you need anything—call me?"

He thought he'd pushed it; she was silent for so long. It was almost as if she'd held her breath—and he wasn't sure if it was fear of him—or awkwardness over the machine.

"Do you think you'll believe me if I say I've seen him again?"

"I do believe you."

"About the slot machine, too, right?" she'd asked dryly.

"I'll believe you. If someone is doing this, seriously, I need to know."

At that, she'd grimaced, and the grimace had turned into a smile. He'd been so tempted to reach out and touch her face and tell her that it was all right.

But was it? Did she have an overactive imagination? No one else had seen a man who appeared to have stepped right out of a portrait.

Whatever it was, she believed it. And when he'd been sitting close to her, their knees just about touching, he knew that he wanted to believe. And, he wanted her to be okay...for no logical reason, he found himself worried about her again. He was reaching at straws.

That, of course, made him determined again that he had to figure out if he was crazy—associated bodies found in three states—or if he was on to something.

"I—uh—I should get up," she'd said at last. "I have appointments in the morning."

"Call me," he'd told her softly. She'd nodded and risen and turned back with a shimmering flow of her long hair. "I don't have your number.

He'd pulled out his phone. "I'll call you, and you'll have it."

He could have just handed her his card.

But, he'd keyed her number into his phone as she gave it to him and let it ring. And she'd smiled and told him, "I've got your number."

Once again, she'd left him.

Once again, she turned back.

"Thank you. The museum was great, and dinner was lovely."

"Any time."

And then, of course, she'd been gone.

He glanced at his phone, at her number, and added her name.

When he looked up, Milt was coming toward him.

"You found something?" he asked. "Catherine Maddox?"

"I haven't found Catherine, I'm afraid. But...I need to spend hours with the videos she appears in during the days she was here. I'm afraid that she may be in serious danger."

"Lady Blue danger?" Milt asked.

Micah nodded. "Exactly. I'll tell you what I've found. Get me back into security."

***

It was impossible for Sienna to not feel like an idiot.

Or worse—what if Micah thought that she'd made it up about the slot machine, maybe even made it up about seeing someone who looked like his ancestor, just to get him to...to come back to the casino.

To spend time with her?

Naturally, Lucy was awake—dressed in her pajamas, seated on the bed, waiting—when she came up to her room.

"Well, well, well?" Lucy said. "Details, down to the juicy bits. I am a married woman now—I have to have all new and exciting wild times through you!"

"Nothing," Sienna said.

"Nothing, not a kiss goodnight—"

"Lucy, I just met him!"

"Yes, but, he's beautiful, you're beautiful, and he's cool, no, super cool, and the way he walks, just this natural thing, and everyone notices him, and you should have both just said, oh, the hell with it, and fallen into one another's arms!"

"Right. In the middle of a casino floor?"

Lucy laughed. "I'm sure it's happened before."

Sienna must have given her a look.

"Oh, come on! You know that you want to jump his bones."

"Is that still even an expression?"

Lucy became serious. "Sienna, he's nice, he's gorgeous, he's...he even smells sexy. Take a chance—if I weren't in love and married and a mom, I'd be...you have to feel it when he's around. The air itself gets masculine by him!"

"He's being kind to two women, and he knows now that you're on a work break from diapers, and he's...you're right. He's kind. I don't think—"

"That's just it. Don't think. Go with it."

Lucy was right; the very air seemed charged when she sat next to him. They'd nearly touched, so close at the machine, and she had felt him there, as if they did. Instinct told her that she should step up to him, step into his arms. That everything would be natural from there.

People didn't act on instinct; they had rules and ethics and morals and...

"Okay, okay, so what about the slot machine?" Lucy demanded.

Sienna shook her head, baffled. "I don't know—I just don't understand it. The cowboy bonus image just wasn't the same. And, I'm not crazy, I did see it this morning, and I did see a guy running around dressed like that. And..."

Her voice trailed. She had forgotten to tell Micah that the man was calling her Eliza, and telling her, "Time to get the bad guys."

"I just thought of something." She said, pulling out her phone.

"You're calling...him?"

"Yes."

"Lord be praised!"

"Nothing like that, I just need to tell him..."

Her voice trailed a second time as he answered. She could hear the ding-ding-ding of a machine. He was still in the casino.

"Sienna, hey, you okay?" he asked anxiously.

"Yes, I just forgot to tell you...this morning, when the image popped up, it said, 'Time to get the bad guys.' And when I saw the man in the museum and at the cemetery, he said the same thing. Oh, and he called me, Eliza."

There was silence on the other end—so long that she thought he'd hung up on her.

But she could still hear the ding-ding-ding that meant he was still in the casino.

"He said what?"

"Time to get the bad guys,'" she repeated, "and he called me—"

"Eliza," he said.

Again, he was silent. She saw that Lucy was staring at her oddly, too.

"What?" she mouthed to her friend.

"He must think you're crazy!" Lucy whispered.

"Why?" She mouthed again.

"At the museum, when we parted way, you went for the history section—I went for myth and legend. You already know that the original Micah's wife was named Eliza. But before he told her to run and that he loved her, his last words were, 'Time to get the bad guys!'"

Sienna started to hang up; she was suddenly cold, stunned, and scared.

He had to think that she was entirely a flake. Or worse again—that she knew about the legend and was creating a thing over it for attention.

He had probably hung up on her.

She certainly would have hung up on someone who sounded the way she did!

How the hell had someone used that name for her, said the exact words...

Then he spoke.

"I'm going to find whoever is doing this, and, I'm so sorry, but, you've got to be careful. Really careful."

"Oh! I guess everyone but me knew about the legend. It must be a...an actor, or someone out to torment me, or you, and..."

"You need to be careful, please, really careful. This is probably something entirely different, but a woman has gone missing, and the body of another—who had gone missing—was found out in the desert long after she'd disappeared. Like I said, it's probably not related, but...just, please, be careful, stay around people."

She felt a ridiculous sense of relief—when she should have been frightened. Not ridiculously frightened, just wary. She'd grown up street-smart, and, since she came from New Orleans—where, it seemed to her, too often people came just to be crazy and commit crimes—she liked to think that she was already alert and wary.

As far as this went...

She was just glad that...he believed her.

"Of course, thank you, I'll be careful."

"I'll see you tomorrow," he said softly.

She didn't question his words; he added a, "Goodnight," and then he was gone, and she couldn't protest, or...

Tell him that yes, please, he must see her.

Because she very much so wanted to see him...

Sienna thought that it would be difficult to sleep that night, but, Lucy was still playing games on her phone when Sienna gave it all up, curled into bed and was quickly out.

Unfortunately, she didn't sleep well; she kept waking up. She was having dreams that were broken and disjointed. The Micah Stratford of old seemed to be with her, and they were walking through a cemetery. "Harder these days," he told her. "You used to know the bad guy—you'd look him right in the face, and because it was hard to be a lawman in lawless times, the bad guy didn't give a whit. Today, you have to look closer."

Then, he'd be gone, and she'd be standing in the cemetery, staring at the man's grave.

Next, the Micah she was coming to know was standing next to her. She could feel the man and breathe in his scent, and she was tempted to remember that she was young and free, and while she liked people, she'd never felt such an urge...

An urge. To what? To pretend that she did know him?

The cemetery seemed to be alive. Ghostly forms were everywhere, seated on the graves here and there, leaning against the monuments.

And Micah Stratford was just there with her, and together, they were staring at the grave. "You have to be careful, please," he told her.

And then, someone else said, "A woman disappeared."

"Ghastly!" came another voice, another of the apparitions in the cemetery. "And yet another was found in a box in the ground, dried and sere, so sad, they say she might have been buried alive."

It was as if the ghosts were having a get-together, talking about the present, sitting around the cemetery, just chatting.

One of the dead looked right at her. "Buried alive!"

She could have sworn that she felt Micah Stratford's arms on her shoulders, like he was determined to keep her safe.

"There's someone running around, taking on different appearances. You have to be careful, so very careful."

She awoke with a start. She was, of course, alone in her bed—with Lucy sleeping just feet away.

But, the dream disturbed her, and she kept remembering when they were in the cemetery, when she saw the man who so resembled the Micah Stratford of years ago.

For some reason, she was thinking of the tour guide as well, the woman who talked about the way soil erosion and more were taking their toll.

With a groan, she tossed and turned. Finally, she managed to get back to sleep. Then, her dreams were haunting in another way.

They were disturbing in a very embarrassing way.

Because she dreamed that she was with him, that he lay next to her, that they were both naked, and in one another's arms.

***

Micah sat in a corner of the security room with Rory Paxton, one of Milt's most trusted security men.

Screens blanketed the walls, and twenty-plus workers watched them.

One section was dedicated to the floor—personnel kept an eager eye on the gaming tables and every once in a while, one of the pit bosses would look at the camera and nod, letting them know that from his end, everything was going well.

The casino had nothing against people winning—they had to pay back at a certain percentage, and, if there wasn't a real possibility of winning, people wouldn't gamble.

He didn't care if they won or lost at the moment. He'd viewed so much of the footage, but, he wasn't something particularly definable—he'd know it when he saw it.

He was certain someone had been stalking Catherine Maddox before she'd disappeared. Someone who had followed her, listened to her chat with other people, and known what her agenda had been.

Catherine Maddox was a tall blond, an attractive woman with a quick smile.

Sienna Johnston was an attractive blond with lovely features and gold-green eyes. She was slim and agile and naturally seductive with her every casual movement, but, her true charm was in her smile, in her way of listening to those around her...

Concentrate.

And then he saw what they had missed, and missed because it was a casino, because people were moving about everywhere.

And the stalker had been a chameleon.

So good at morphing from one appearance to another, it was difficult to tell if it was a man, or a woman.

He first realized what he was seeing because of the housekeeper who had headed into Catherine Maddox's room. Either a very big woman—or a man, dressed as a woman.

He backtracked the trail of the maid, but she had arrived at the casino in uniform, had gone through the service entrance, and picked up her cart.

There were, of course, so many housekeepers at the casino that on any given day, one might well be working with different people—and new people.

He studied the movements of the person, and then looked at the casino floor. He was certain that the maid, re-dressed, was a man in a hoodie, following Catherine Maddox as she went for coffee the following day, and then paused to lose a few dollars in a machine.

Catherine seemed to be—*he prayed that he could still speak of her in present tense*—apparently a nice person. She lost money, shrugged, smiled, and appeared to tell someone near her to have good luck.

He could be wrong, but he didn't think so. There was no way to really study the face of the person he was certain he saw several times—the next appearance was in a feminine dress suit—and a huge hat that hung over the head.

It wasn't much to go on; he could study these forever, but, he could also bring in some experts—cops who specialized in computer statistics, marking height, weight, and more than just movement.

"Rory, will you look at what I'm seeing?" Micah asked.

"Sure. Okay, a hefty maid, a guy in a hoodie—oh, wait, dozens of guys in hoodies—and a lady all dressed up for dinner. Big girl, huh?"

"Maybe not," Micah said.

"Oh, oh, oh! I see what you mean," Rory said, drawing a chair up to study the images again, backwards and forwards through days of surveillance in the hall and on the elevator, and on the casino floor.

"We'll call Milt," Rory said.

"And the cops," Micah advised. "I know we both have friends working on this; it will be important for them to see this, and for me to see what they've got. My feeling is that, if we put all this together, we may just find something. Something, and one can pray,   to   help   us   find   Catherine   Maddox.   Alive."

Chapter 5

Sienna had a dedicated room for her videos, set up with her camera, and what she hoped was a charming background with "Book Your Table" written on it amid books and cover art in a variety of genres.

She had just finished interviewing one of her favorite sci-fi authors when there was a knock at the door. It opened partially, then completely, and she looked up from the desk where she'd been studying her most recent interview on her computer screen.

It was Micah Stratford. To her annoyance, her heartbeat quickened, and something else inside of her seemed to take flight.

"Have a minute?" he asked.

She did; her next interview was with a very popular mystery writer, but she wasn't due for another fifteen minutes.

Everything was all set up, camera ready, mics ready—all set. Ernie—from downstairs in the coffee shop—had set her up with a nice box of coffee, creamers, and sugar—real and fake—and she'd arranged the basic small conference room into something a little more comfortable.

At the moment, she was just sitting—drinking coffee at the table.

"Um, sure," she murmured, and then she smiled. "Do you work at your place—or here, at the casino?"

He shrugged. "I grew up around here, and several people I went to school with now have jobs with the casino. But, in this case, I don't mean to scare you, but...I'm worried about you."

"Oh, um, would you like some coffee?"

"No, thanks. Like I said, I'm a little worried." He cast his head ruefully to the side. "Old cop thing kicking in, I guess."

"Why? I mean, other than that you're a nice guy and you'd worry about anyone. I mean is it because it seems someone has been kidnapped."

He took a chair opposite her at the table.

"I've been reviewing casino tape. We're trying to find out if someone was stalking Catherine Maddox—the woman who has disappeared—and, I believe that someone was. Someone who can take on different identities, wear wigs, appear to be male—and female."

"The person I've been seeing is very definitely male," Sienna said.

"Whatever the appearance this person takes on, it's very real. I believe it is a man—the size would suggest so, or a very tall and hefty woman. I just wish that I'd seen your man."

He didn't say the words as if he doubted her. She lowered her head, thinking that was a small miracle.

She'd felt like such an idiot at the slot machine the night before. And yet, she knew what she'd seen the first time she'd played the machine.

"I wish you'd seen him, too," she said.

"I'm going to try to find him, I think he might be the person we're looking for," he told her. "And I know you're busy here, but, please, this is imperative—if you see him again, please, call me right away."

"Of course," she told him. "I'm in here most of the day, except for one panel. Then there's a movie being shown tonight, but, I'm not sure I am going to go. Lucy is in a panel now, but..."

Her voice trailed. She was about to say that they'd be together. She wasn't sure that they would be—Lucy had a "concept" dinner with an author she'd worked with several times before who wanted to start a series of books, and, needed something about the cover to tie them all together. She was invited, of course—Lucy was a loyal friend.

But, she didn't intend to go.

"Do you have dinner plans?" he asked her.

"Vague ones," she murmured.

"If it's not something you're keen on doing, perhaps you'd come out with me—somewhere near the hotel. Perhaps, if this person is...following you, he might make an appearance. Lucy, too, of course, if she'd like."

"She has a business dinner," Sienna said. "And I..."

"I don't want to keep you from anything," he said.

There was a tap at the door again; B.J. Carlyle, the mystery writer she'd been expecting, popped her head in. "Hey, Sienna, you ready for me?" She paused, looking at Micah. "Oh, I'm sorry—I don't mean to interrupt."

"You're not interrupting; I'm on way out, but, thank you," Micah said. "Sienna?"

She wanted to go. She knew if she didn't she would go home, and she would wonder what might have been had she just taken a chance.

He wasn't exactly asking her out for pleasure—he'd fairly frankly said that he was taking her out as bait.

"Sure, fine. What time?" she asked.

"You tell me," he said.

"Six, six-thirty—seven?"

"Six-thirty," he said, and, nodding politely to B.J., he exited the room after holding the door for her to enter.

B.J. was staring at him. Sienna cleared her throat. "B.J., I'd like you to meet Micah Stratford. Micah, one of the world's most wonderful mystery writers, B.J. Carlyle."

Micah smiled and shook B.J.'s hand. "I have some of your novels. You are a wonderful writer," he assured her.

B.J. was always blunt. She grinned and stared back at him. "And you—you're just wonderful!" she told him.

"Thank you—a pleasure," he said, and then he was gone.

"Oh, my," B.J. said. "Sienna, is he with you? What an incredible looking man—I have to have him as a character in a book. I mean, he is unique. A bit of a cowboy, a bit of a steampunk hero. So, who is he? When did you meet him? When did you start dating? Are you—"

"He's a man I just met—he runs a little museum, a really great little museum, out between here and Virginia City. And, see, he knows that you are an incredible writer," Sienna said, changing the subject. "So, the camera is set—I ask questions, but you're on the video alone and I edit out my questions. It's just as if you're talking to readers, and we'll have it run two minutes. I really want to thank you for doing this for me—I know you're asked to do many major interviews."

"I get to be in a restaurant in New Orleans full time—I'm all for it!" B.J. said. As she took her chair, though, she was looking toward the door.

"I'm going to have to go to that museum!" B.J. said.

***

When he left Sienna, Micah headed straight to the police station. He'd called Artie Flannigan and was grateful that Artie was glad to hear from him.

"You think it's happening again?" Artie had asked on the phone.

"I don't think this guy has stopped; I think he moves around—all in the near enough vicinity—and that he struck here again."

"Hell, I hope not."

Micah and Artie were old friends—teammates from back in college. Micah was also friends with Artie's captain, Joseph Murdock—Murdock had spent a few summers as a trail guide for Micah's dad when Murdock had been in high school and Micah had been a pain-in-the-ass five-year-old, wanting to follow Murdock everywhere.

When he arrived at the station, he was greeted by several of the cops, and then led to a conference room where Artie and Joseph were set up with a tech, ready to show him video they'd pulled from bank and other surveillance cameras.

"You really think we can find our man this way?" Murdock asked him.

"I think we can maybe see if I'm right and we do have someone who can change his spots in the wink of an eye—I can't tell just how much video I've gone through already. This guy is a chameleon—he can become anyone. That way, he can stalk someone without being noted. Like I said, I believe that this guy is local, that he's the one who kidnapped Lady Blue and several other women in the region."

"Why don't we know about him?" Murdock asked.

"Because, it's taken so long to find the bodies, and they're disposed of so differently, that his crimes haven't been connected. I also want to believe that we could be in time—that Catherine Maddox might still be alive, but if so...we have to find her fast."

Artie glanced at his captain, and Murdock glanced back. He thought that they might be questioning his use of the word "we."

Murdock simply said, "Thank you—if this helps, hell, you might be the one to save a life. Again."

Micah winced.

Yes, I saved lives, and I lost them, too.

"May I see anything you have?" he asked, changing the subject.

They all sat for about ten minutes. Bank cameras could catch a lot; they saw Catherine Maddox walking down a street. They saw her looking at a window display.

They saw her coming up to an ATM for a withdrawal, and, it was during that shot of her that Micah stiffened and sat up. "There!" he said, pointing. Right there, standing back a bit." He looked at them dryly. "The nun, lighting a cigarette. That's him—or her. The costumes keep you from knowing, but the size suggests male. I've watched the casino videos, and since the look changes so completely every time, I studied movement. There, even in the habit, when he moves away from the ATM, you can see that he favors his left side." He glanced at Captain Murdock. "If I remember right, you have a great tech officer who can do specs on this and give us an idea of the height and other factors regarding this person. Milt is getting together everything we found from the casino surveillance."

"It could just be an ugly nun," Murdock murmured. "Not implying that nuns may or may not be ugly, but, that one...I guess it could be a man."

"But, do we know that he took Catherine?" Artie murmured. "This person you're seeing could definitely be a very strange kook, but..."

"Wait—there," Murdock said.

Catherine Maddox turned away from the ATM and almost ran straight into the nun. The nun caught her by the shoulders. Smiled.

There was something about that smile...

They could see, when Catherine Maddox broke away, there was something about her, as well. Something new in her eyes.

Fear.

***

"So, you're not coming to dinner with me?" Lucy asked. She looked perplexed. "It could be good, and I don't like to think of you running around—oh, wait, did you make other dinner plans? With authors—marketers?"

Lucy must have read something in Sienna's eyes because she gasped suddenly. "Oh, oh, ooh! You saw him, he called you, and you're going to dinner with him. I am so proud of you!"

"Don't get carried away—he's concerned about the man I keep seeing. He believes that there is someone taking on different guises, and that the person might now be imitating his ancestor—I'm guessing that there are copies of that picture of Micah Stratford we saw at the museum in guide books, or history books. He was supposedly something of a local hero. Add to that, a woman's body was found in a box in the desert, and another woman has disappeared, so...he's worried."

"About you!"

"And others, of course."

"Catherine Maddox—that woman who's missing." Lucy shook her head. "She's probably dead."

"Lucy."

"I'm being realistic. Anyway, especially under these circumstances, make sure that you text me if you decide to stay out for the night."

"I'm not staying out for the night," Sienna said.

Lucy grinned. "Well, you're not bringing him back here—not with me in the room!"

"Lucy!"

"Hey, come on, have a life, have some fun, do something wild and crazy and daring!"

Sienna ignored the comment and glanced at her watch. "He should be here; I'm heading back down to the entrance to meet him. And you—you be careful! This is not a good situation, and you have a beautiful little boy at home, so, you have to watch out for yourself."

"I'll be very careful," Lucy said. "Oh, you're going out with Micah. That's so delightful."

"You also have a beautiful husband," Sienna reminded her.

"Yes, and that's why I'll be living vicariously through you!"

Sienna grinned, waved, and left the room.

As she walked down the hallway alone, she was a little afraid that the impersonator of the Micah Stratford of old was going to pop out of one of the other rooms.

She made it to the elevator fine. Of course, she knew that there were cameras watching in the halls, and in the elevator—

but, what good was a camera if something was happening in the now? Could security get there quickly enough?"

Nothing is going to happen to me in the hall or the elevator, she told herself.

And nothing did.

She reached the front of the casino, an area teeming with people. Micah had already arrived and was leaning against his car, talking with one of the valets. He smiled when he saw her, stood straight, and walked around to open the passenger side door for her.

"Thanks for this," he told her.

"My pleasure—just trying to figure out if I'm a worm on a hook, or chum, or..."

"A star witness," he told her. "You're the only one who has seen him—or her—in this guise."

"But, you said that he—or she—changes all the time. So, wouldn't he be on to a different disguise or personae by now?"

"Possibly, but—you saw him or her in that costume or disguise several times already. It might be something that he's playing with, or..."

"He might be targeting me."

"Never hurts to be careful."

"I agree," she murmured. "So, now?"

He shrugged. "Dinner. Thought we'd head out to Casale's Halfway Club—so named," he added with a grin, "because it's halfway between Sparks and Reno. It started out as a fruit stand—not elegant, but...there's elegant in all the casinos. It's historic and intriguing."

"I love it!" she told him honestly.

From the moment they arrived, she really did love the place. Micah told her that it was one of the oldest restaurants in the area, and the only one continually owned by one family. It was charming, with old wine bottles hanging from rafters above the bar, checkered table cloths, and, certainly a boon, some of the most incredible Italian food Sienna had ever eaten.

As they finished their meals, Sienna turned the discussion to Micah. "I'm curious; a hotel security man called you for help—

because Catherine Maddox disappeared, and she was at the casino. And you also have friends within the police force."

"I was a cop for a while, in Chicago, like I told you and Lucy."

"Okay? Right, but, you came back here, and then...you didn't join the force here, but, you're still friends with the cops—and work with them?"

He shrugged. "I grew up here. Back in Chicago, there was a really bad situation—a bank heist. We saved a lot of hostages, and we lost a few. Drove me a little crazy. Anyway, maybe I needed the break. My family had the property here. I grew up here. And, yeah, I still have tons of friends here. My dad needed to move on—my mother passed away a long time ago, and he's finally remarried." Micah smiled. "They're in Hawaii. So, I hate to admit it, but, I did have a bad time after that heist, so when I got the phone call from my father at about the same time, it just seemed right to come home. But, I can't help being drawn back to law enforcement now and then. There are just days when you can make a difference, and days when you can't, and days in which, even if you make a difference, there's a lot of loss. I need to determine if I can live with myself during the losses as well as the times when you have really good results. I may want to move on, but, only after my family heritage is up and running in good shape. Of course, I have great people working for me and I'm not a micro-manager, so, I could move on at some point."

"Hotel security?"

"No!" he protested, and then laughed. "Sorry—security is incredibly important, and those working that kind of detail definitely deal with some scary individuals. They also deal with far too many drunks, weepy ones, partying ones—and drunks who just get mad because they believe someone threw the dice badly. Milt is great at his job—he knows how to handle people. He can see clearly if something is a minor disturbance that needs to be quietly handled, and when there's a real problem and you need the police. Anyway, I've thought about a few venues, but, I'm still focused on the museum and figuring out if I'm staying here or moving on. What about you? An artist/restaurant owner?"

"My restaurant isn't due to open for a few more months," she told him. She grimaced. "I grew up in New Orleans. Even as a little kid, I'd walk around Jackson Square just to see all the new artists and everything going on. I loved to sketch, and my mom and dad thought I was good—of course, your parents always think you're good—but, they got me into magnet schools and then a great art school, and I still love every aspect of art. Especially when it comes to books. I love to read. I also know that people are essentially visual—they will pick up a book with a great cover. People rushing through an airport will stop—if a cover attracts them. When you're just making your way through an airport or grocery store or pharmacy, your mind isn't usually on buying a book, but, if art attracts you—you will stop. Lucy is really the cover artist, though, and I support her whole-heartedly."

"Your family is in New Orleans?"

"Some are in Ibiza, some in New Orleans, but...yes, from the area."

"Your ex has left the city, and you're not seeing anyone, right?"

Sienna felt her jaw drop. "I—"

"Lucy filled me in," he supplied quickly.

"Great. I wasn't married, we were just seeing each other a long time, and then you realize one day that...you've gone in different directions. He wasn't a horrible person or anything; we just changed."

He smiled. "You want to make sure you're not even edging on someone else's toes," he said quietly. "Me—in my case," he added with a smile, "everything went to hell in Chicago. My fault. I couldn't concentrate—I was terrible. Moral dilemmas all around. Anyway, back to New Orleans. It's definitely a food mecca," he said.

Sienna wasn't sure what he said then; she looked up, outside, and a light caught on something.

It was him. The cowboy.

She leaned forward. "He's outside. I just saw him walk by."

Micah stood in a second flat, tossed a wad of bills on the table, and hurried outside. He must have eaten at the restaurant fairly frequently; he apparently knew the menu and the prices. Sienna raced after him.

"Which way?" Micah asked.

"I don't know—but, he was here, I swear it!"

They stood on the sidewalk by a sign that announced, "Since 1937," and then, "Ravioli, Lasagna, and More." He turned to her. "Stay. Right here—by the restaurant door, with dozens of people. Do not let anyone take you anywhere. You understand? Stay, don't move!"

He headed off down the street.

People were coming and going, singly, in twos and threes and more. Neon blinked, people smiled, they were polite, excusing themselves as they walked by her. She watched as Micah hurried down the street, and then disappeared into a crowd.

She turned, and the man—the original Micah from the old photograph—was there, right behind her.

He didn't try to touch her.

"Eliza!" he said softly, all but choking with emotion. "It's you...I see you so clearly, I know it's you, I've searched, I've waited, but...Finally. You see me. And I think...I think it's all about life. Chances. Maybe...the terraces, the cemetery, Eliza, maybe, I can hope, if we save others...can you hear me, my love? You see me, I know that you see me!"

Her mouth worked; she was stunned, and scared. "Please, please, stay here. Please help. Did you take her? Did you bury Catherine Maddox? Please..."

"No! Me? God no, I would never...But, I saw the earth, I saw the ground. And maybe..."

"Sienna!"

She heard her name called. Micah was hurrying back toward her. She looked his way, reaching out to hold on to his great-great-grandfather's doppelganger, but she grasped air. She turned back; he was gone.

Chapter 6

Micah hurried back, instantly worried; Sienna's face told him that she was both stunned and scared.

"He...he was here. Right here, behind me. Now he's gone again."

"Did he hurt you?" Micah asked anxiously.

"No, no—"

"Did he threaten you in anyway?"

"No—he called me Eliza again. He said that maybe if we helped...and he mentioned the cemetery."

"Cemetery?" Micah demanded.

She nodded, hair tumbled around her shoulders, eyes wide. "Cemeteries—outside Virginia City, I think. That's where I saw him before. I mean, one of the times before—Micah, do you think that he is the kidnapper...killer?"

Micah was already on the phone—he'd slipped a calming arm around her, but he apparently had someone on speed dial.

He glanced down at her. "The cemetery—near my family plot?" he asked her.

"Yes...um, a guide was pointing out erosion and other natural influences that were causing damage to the cemeteries."

He hung up.

"You good?" he asked her, taking her by the shoulders and looking into her eyes. "He just found you; I can't leave you alone right now. You understand."

"I'm okay, but...but..."

"I have to get out to the terraces, to the cemeteries."

"It's night, it's dark...how can you—"

"The police and the FBI are meeting us out there. Are you all right? Can you come with me?"

He was right about one thing—she didn't want to be here alone. Not when the psycho actor was out here somewhere.

"Can I? Of course."

She wanted to sound strong.

A cemetery.

In the middle of the night.

"Of course," she repeated, and she managed what she hoped was the semblance of a smile. "But, what if he was wrong, what if it was just a come on to see what I would do—to see what you would do?"

"And what if Catherine Maddox is in the ground—with only hours or minutes of oxygen to go?" he asked softly. "What if..."

He didn't finish the thought.

They both knew that Catherine Maddox might already be dead.

***

Micah could remember his father telling him once, when he'd been a child and nervous visiting a graveyard, that the dead were the safest people in the world to be around. They didn't wield guns or knives, and were, hopefully, at rest.

Even if a ghost jumped out of the ground, what was he going to do?

Then, of course, he'd heard the presidential speech by Franklin Delano Roosevelt—very important to remember in a cemetery, and in a cemetery, especially— "The only thing we have to fear is fear itself."

A cop friend later amended that by adding, "Unless you're chasing a drug dealer through the cemetery, or something like that!"

Micah didn't think there were any drug runners conducting deals on the terraces that night. It was just about dead still when they arrived, and when they did, the cops were already there.

Captain Joseph Murdock had arrived, along with Detective Artie Flannigan. Police and forensic techs were busy, running machinery over ragged, scruff and the barren steps of the area.

Micah introduced the detective and his captain to Sienna.

"So, you're the young lady our possible suspect has been hounding?" Artie asked her.

"I'm not sure hounding is right, and, he might just be a kook," Sienna told them quickly. She was shivering slightly.

There just was something about a cemetery in the darkness.

"But, he suggested to you that that there might be someone in the cemetery?" Artie asked.

She nodded. "I—I hope, sir, that I haven't dragged everyone out at night for a wild goose chase," Sienna said. "But, I have seen this man several times."

"And he's probably a killer," Artie said.

"I don't think so, but, I think he might have seen the killer. He vehemently denied being the killer, and keeps calling me Eliza, and seems elated that I see him—although he manages to disappear anytime he might be seen by someone else," Sienna said.

She was speaking firmly and easily, and still, he saw that she was shivering, miserable.

He slipped an arm around her shoulder. "I'm thinking someone should get Sienna back to her hotel—and safely to her room," he said.

She shook her head vehemently. "No, no, thank you. I need to...I dragged everyone out here, though I'm not sure I meant to, but...no, I'll stay. If it's all right, if I may," she added.

She'd barely spoken before someone working on one of the terrace "steps" gave a shout-out. "Hey, could be old and shifted, but I'm getting a strong signal here, and..."

There was a general hustle of movement that drowned out whatever else he'd been going to say. He, Artie, and Captain Murdock all made a move instantly, running over to where the tech was standing.

"Shovels," Murdock ordered.

They were quickly supplied.

It was a cemetery. Coffins and bodies had been shifting for a century-plus.

They might have found anything; they might be digging up the old bones of a miner.

"I've hit wood—a wooden box!" Someone shouted, and the workers became more frenzied, shoveling out earth, grass tufts, pebbles...and then, finding that box.

An old coffin? One that hadn't deteriorated and broken down with time? One that would contain old bones and bit and pieces of a life lost and gone on by.

"Don't crack it, don't crush it," Artie Flannigan warned.

"Crack the thing—it's...it's new, looks new, pine, a pine box..." a tech said.

The box was lifted out of the ground.

"Heavy!" Someone grunted.

The box was out of the ground; someone was quickly there with a crow bar, jerking up the simple lid, which had been nailed on.

And, inside...

Captain Murdock swore.

Micah moved forward, anxiously looking into the coffin. And, there she was. The woman he had seen in the footage from the casino, and the ATM, and other cameras. She was twisted and turned, as if she had struggled desperately to free herself, desperately trying anything for air...

There was also something in the coffin with her. An oxygen tank. Her kidnapper had left her with a small supply of air...

He started to reach into the box.

"No, no—no one can touch her until the M.E. gets here," Artie warned quickly.

"M.E.?" Micah protested. "She might be alive." Micah said.

Murdock was already in action; within minutes, uniformed rescue workers were on the scene, one speaking to the hospital and a doctor, another working with oxygen and setting up an I.V.

In the middle of the action, Micah remembered that Sienna was there; he panicked, looking around, thinking she might have hurried down to them when the shouting had begun.

She was not; he searched and saw her.

She was standing where he'd left her, framed by the moon, almost a mystical site as the night breeze played with her hair. He hurried back over to her, looking at her curiously. She seemed almost frozen, as if a ghost had walked up to her and said, "Boo."

"Sienna?" he asked softly.

Her voice was barely a whisper as she asked, "She's alive?"

"Yes, for now. I don't get it—the other woman was found with nothing. He had left Catherine Maddox with a tank of oxygen. It's out...if we hadn't found her tonight, she wouldn't have made it."

Sienna was pale; she became even whiter—if possible—in the moonlight.

"She's—alive?" she whispered.

"Thanks to you," he told her softly.

She shook her head, confused, and then said, "No...not me. The...man. The man who looks like your ancestor. But, if he dresses up...and he's the one who put her there, why would he have told me to look here? It is a miracle that she was found. Alive," she added on a breath.

"She's unconscious, barely breathing, and we have to pray that she makes it," Micah said, "but, yes, it's something of a miracle. I believe the kidnapper was giving Catherine—or us—a chance. Maybe, when she comes to, she'll be able to tell us what happened to her."

Maybe. And maybe not. She might have been jumped from behind, drugged, coerced—or taken by a kidnapper/killer in a guise impossible to trace.

By then, Captain Murdock and Artie had made their way over to where Micah stood with Sienna.

"Can you tell us anything about the man who approached you on the street, Sienna?" Captain Murdock asked. "Describe him for a police artist?"

"I really don't need to do that," Sienna said. "If you go to Micah's museum, you can see a picture of him."

"Whoever this is, he's now dressing up as the original Micah Stratford," Micah said.

"To a T," Sienna whispered.

"And he's approached you several times now?" Murdock asked, frowning.

"At the museum, here in the cemetery, on the street," Sienna said.

"Can you tell us anything else about him?" Artie asked. "Pattern of speech? Anything?"

Sienna looked very strange—still scared, uneasy, and, the strangest, unwilling to talk.

"Isn't he really playing the role?" Micah asked quietly. "Calling you by my ancestor's name?"

"Yes, he calls me 'Eliza,'" she said. It was as if she was suddenly unwilling to admit what she had just said, and really didn't want to talk about her encounters at all.

"She needs a security detail," Artie said.

"No," she said quietly. "I don't need a security detail."

"This man is evidently stalking you, and we need to catch him," Murdock said.

She suddenly seemed to come to, smiling at Murdock and speaking calmly, clearly, and rationally. "Captain Murdock, I'm staying at a casino. There are cameras everywhere. Unless you want an officer sharing a room with my friend and me, it's not likely it would help any."

"You do leave the casino," Artie reminded her.

"I can make sure I'm there—Milt can give me a room on the same floor," Micah said. "I can be there if Sienna wants to leave the hotel."

"You're not on the payroll, Micah," Murdock said. "Wouldn't mind if you were, but...honestly, we don't offer this often, Sienna. We don't have the manpower for it. We do have a safe house, but, unless Catherine Maddox does survive and tell us, we have no more leads on this man."

"Maybe there will be forensics...or the box will tell us something. That was a box she was found in, not a coffin. It had to have been constructed somewhere," Micah said.

Captain Murdock looked at them all. "Micah, if you're right and these unsolved murders here and in surrounding states have been perpetrated by the same killer, he hasn't left a clue. I'm sure he's wearing some kind of gloves. They haven't had anything at all to connect a killer to any of the crimes—not a fiber. This just isn't safe." He turned to Sienna. "Perhaps you should go home—forget whatever this business is."

She shook her head. "If the man approaching me is the killer, and if Micah doesn't mind being something of a watchdog for a few days...I might be your only link."

Artie sighed. "I don't think you realize—"

"I'm not leaving," Sienna said flatly. "Not while my convention is still on."

"Stubborn. Stubborn and foolish," Murdock warned her.

"And maybe our only chance," Artie murmured.

"For now, let me get you back—straight to your door. Which, of course, you'll immediately lock," Micah told her. "And I'll get with Milt; he'll fix things up."

"As you wish. We're going to get over to the hospital now. There could be a miracle. Miss Maddox might wake up and solve the whole thing for us," Murdock said.

"Right," Artie murmured.

Micah slipped an arm around Sienna's shoulders and led her out of the cemetery, back to where he'd parked his car. She didn't speak as they walked.

And, she didn't speak once they were in the car.

"Sienna, this is dangerous. I know this is business for you, but, maybe, you should go home. This man is stalking you," he told her.

She was looking straight ahead as he drove.

"He's no danger to me," she said.

"How can you say that? He's approached you over, and over."

She turned to look at him. "He's really no danger to me," she repeated.

"And why is that?"

"Because...because,   he's   dead   himself."

Chapter 7

Sienna had to wonder if he was going to want to protect her once he heard what she had to say.

She wasn't sure that she believed what had happened herself.

She'd seen the police and the technicians, seen them find the box in the earth, and then...

He'd been there next to her, Micah Stratford, just as she'd seen him in the slot machine, at the museum, in the cemetery before...and on the street that night. She hadn't heard him come; he'd just suddenly been there. Staring, with her, at the action taking place on the little step or terrace far beneath them. The moon had rained a glow down upon them, and it had been an eerie thing, standing there among the tombstones.

"Maybe...maybe..." he had whispered first. "Eliza, maybe there's a reason for it all. You're here...I see you. And you see me. Maybe she will live."

Then, as if the moon blinked and there was a split second of darkness, he disappeared within that strange moment.

Of course, she could be in need of serious psychological counseling.

But...

No. She was sane. She'd seen him appear on the slot machine—where a different image appeared later. And he'd approached her in the museum. He was real—and he was dead.

Of course, after saying such a thing to Micah, she received the worried glance she'd expected, and gentle words. He spoke the way you might speak to a child—or a crazy person.

"You've been under tremendous stress, and, to my sorrow, I'm sure I've certainly added to it. And, thanks to you seeing the man, we did find Catherine Maddox."

"We don't know how long she was without oxygen," Sienna said, hoping that she sounded perfectly logical and clear. "I'm hoping we didn't save her to live another few years in a state of vegetation."

"We'll know more soon. But, I don't think that you realize the danger in this situation. You think that a ghost has come back to...to stalk you, but, he can't really hurt you—because he's a ghost."

"I don't think; it's the truth," she said flatly. She turned to him as he drove. "There may be a dozen people in this city dressing up as your ancestor and stalking people, maybe even kidnapping and killing them. But, the man I'm seeing is dead."

He let that go for a few minutes.

"Did you see him tonight? Did you see any time?" Sienna asked. "No, and, he was in the slot machine—that's the first time I saw him. I don't know how the hell it works, but, he was there. What? Do you think I knew where she was because I buried her? I have witnesses by the scores who will swear that I was in New Orleans when she disappeared."

"Sienna, Sienna, I know you saw a man. I know that he spoke to you. But, he's good. He can disappear in a flash. He knows the city, knows how to play it—"

"He disappeared in front of my eyes."

"A trick of the moonlight."

Had it been? No! She knew what she saw.

She turned away from him, looking straight ahead as he drove. "Please, don't bother getting a room. I'll be fine—and I don't want you watching over me."

"I'll be getting a room," he said flatly. "And, I will be watching over you."

"I don't want you watching over me."

"I'm sorry; that's too bad. You're a link to the killer."

"Do what you want then—but, don't expect me to make anything easy for you."

"Sienna..."

"I know what I know," she said simply.

When they arrived, she was out of the car as soon as he drove up to the valet. She thought she could run in and escape him—he'd have to give the valet his keys.

She's forgotten he seemed to know too many of the valet drivers. He just tossed his keys to a young man with a nod and came hurrying after her.

She headed for the elevator, producing her room key.

The security man by the elevator allowed her in, and then nodded at Micah as he followed her; she rued the fact that the man seemed to know everyone.

She pressed the number to her floor, and then, when the elevator reached her level, she pushed the button for "Casino Floor."

"I suddenly have a mad desire to play craps," she said.

"Fine."

The elevator reached the ground. She gritted her teeth and pushed the button for her floor again; she was exhausted, and she was a mess. She wasn't sure she even wanted to see Lucy right then, because, of course, Lucy would think that she was crazy, too, if she tried to explain.

But, she needed sleep.

They reached her floor again and he walked her to her door. "There are cameras, you know, in the hallways and the elevator," he said. "If you're in any trouble, make sure you don't let anyone push you back into your room. Get into the hallway and scream bloody murder."

She nodded, slipping her key into the lock. She was on edge and distraught—that was the only excuse for what she said next.

"Too bad you proved to be such an ass. I was thinking about sleeping with you tonight."

Her door opened; she stepped in and closed it as quickly as possible.

She hoped that Lucy wasn't back in the room yet; she was, of course. It was well after midnight.

"Sienna! You came back!"

"Of course, I came back."

"Oh, no daring, no chances—no future, if you don't take the plunge," Lucy said. She was in bed, in her pajamas, but, she'd left the television on. "Did you hear the news? They found her—buried alive! Can you imagine how horrible? How absolutely horrible. She's alive right now, and the hospital has announced her condition as critical."

Sienna wasn't sure how she had such a readable face, but, apparently, she did. Either that, or Lucy knew her too well.

"Oh, my God," Lucy continued. "You know... you know because you were with Micah, and you two were there when she was found?"

"Yes."

"How? How the hell did you...spill! What happened? What the hell happened? The only person talking to the media so far has been a man named Captain Murdock. Cool looking older dude. He said that an anonymous tip led the police to the cemetery. You were the anonymous tip!"

"He came up to me again," Sienna murmured.

"Oh! Oh, Sienna—this guy could be the murderer. And he could be after you! This is serious. We need to leave Reno, right now, pack our bags and get out of here."

"I'm not going anywhere."

"You're crazy! What—did one of us suddenly become an amazing martial artist? Are we 'packing?' What are we going to do if someone does come after you?"

"We're not alone—we're being watched by someone who is 'packing,'" Sienna told her. "Micah Stratford is taking a room down the hall."

Lucy didn't reply with an "Oh," or any words to the effect.

She still looked worried.

"Sienna, I don't know, this is...hey, okay, you're not worried for yourself, but, what about me? I'm here with you. And, as you reminded me, I'm a mom to a little boy!"

That was true—and the best thing Lucy could have said to worry her and make her question what she felt she had to do—stay. See it through.

She sank down to the foot of her bed, afraid, and yet determined.

"I'm going to leave the conference," she said.

"That's probably smartest—we'll both miss out on a lot, but, hey—your life is more important than videos. The rooms in the restaurant just won't have video. They can have pictures, theme prizes, and, of course, books, books being the most important element in the equation!"

Sienna shook her head. "No, you can stay, and I'll be gone, and you won't be in danger that way. Once I'm out of the picture..."

She started to dial and ask to be connected to Micah's room, and then she pulled out her cell phone instead.

He answered before the first ring had completed. "Micah, is there somewhere you can put me up out at your property."

"Yes, of course. You want to come out there?"

"I should be safe there—right?"

"You'll be safe—as long as you stay with me. You saw this guy in the museum. He obviously gets around."

"I'll stay with you."

"You should go home, to New Orleans."

"No. So?"

"We'll leave here in the morning and head out. Unless you want me to be a cameraman, door greeter, or something else. Except, if there is a call from the police, we'll have to go."

"Deal." She hesitated. "You are still here, right? In the hotel."

"Actually, I'm at the desk—I will be right next door."

She opted against a wisecrack at the moment, even though he didn't believe her, didn't believe that she was seeing a dead man.

"Thank you," she said simply.

***

It was a miracle that Catherine Maddox was alive—everyone said it, from the cops to the med techs and the doctors.

A miracle.

Of course, they didn't know yet if she'd suffered brain damage, and no, they couldn't talk to her yet. Because of damage done, she was in a medically induced coma as the doctors worked to rehydrate her and do their best to keep her organs healthy.

Micah wasn't alone as he stood in the hallway at the hospital—he was keeping Sienna with him as much as possible.

She'd been scheduled to do interviews that day, but, Lucy— who had new roommate, another young woman at the hotel who'd been alone, but was now unnerved by events—was going to do the interviews, with the help of a hotel tech—assigned, thankfully, by Milt.

Milt was beyond himself with relief that Catherine had been found alive.

He was also beside himself with worry that they still had no idea of who had taken her.

Until Catherine was talking...

It would only be a matter of days; the doctors had assured them.

"Whoever your kook is, he had to have knowledge of who did this. If he comes anywhere near you again, we have to snag him immediately. I do say though, whether he denied it or not," Artie said, "this dress-up guy of yours sounds like he is the culprit."

Micah watched Sienna; she wasn't about to tell Artie or anyone else that she was pretty sure that her "dress-up guy" was a ghost.

It was while they were standing there, though, that Micah became convinced that whoever was guilty had the ability to come and go from casino without being noted. Also, while someone might go into a public restroom and change clothing and appearance, it would still be difficult to walk in as one sex and out as another.

If that was the case, it seemed most likely that whoever was culpable was either a regular at the hotel and casino—or an employee. Someone who knew the place well enough to know where they wouldn't stand out.

He didn't say anything to Artie yet; he was going to go back over video himself. He'd noted the way the person walked. Now, he had focus on that walk as he re-watched the tapes for anyone and everyone he saw frequently at the hotel.

"All right; I'm taking Sienna out to my place, and then we'll be going back to the casino, and from there, I'll go through video again. Something has to click," Micah said.

"We can hope," Artie said dully. "Hey, the captain said to remind you that you've got a job with us when you want one again, though, hey, maybe we should be asking you, Miss Johnston," he told Sienna.

She smiled weakly.

As they left, she said softly, "Thank you."

"For?"

"Not making me sound like a wanna-be psychic or something—or telling him that I'm convinced that I see the dead."

"Hey, you tell people what you want. It's not up to me."

"But, you really don't believe me."

He hesitated, trying to hide his thoughts. Of course, he didn't believe her. He was a hardened guy who had been through a hell of a lot.

But, on the other hand...

He could have sworn that someone whispered to him when he'd found the dead girl after the hikers had called in about the bone.

It was just my mind at work, he thought.

Still, something had told him where to look.

"Let's drop your suitcase off at my place, and then we'll get back to the casino and the security videos. He's got to be in there somewhere. Of course, you can work if you need to—as long as there are a jillion other people around."

She smiled. "Trust me—I don't want to be buried in a box."

When they reached Micah's place, he didn't head to the museum at first, but, showed Sienna the room he planned for her. It was a single room—just past his room. There was no entry to it past his room, but she'd have her own space.

"It's nice and perfect and this is super of you—but why do you have a little room there?" she asked him. "Was it a—dressing room?"

"I don't think that they built dressing rooms back then," he told her. He added dryly, "Not in the socio-economic group my great-great-great grandfather was in when he moved out here. I'm pretty sure it was planned as a nursery."

"Ah, well that makes sense," she assured him. He set her bag at the foot of the bed and said, "I'd like to head into the museum, if you don't mind. See if the pictures there will...I don't know, bring the original Micah back?"

She nodded. "Sure. And thank you."

"No, I'm really glad you're here, and really glad you're letting me watch over you—until you go home."

She shook her head. "No, sorry, yes—I mean, thank you for watching over me, and getting me away from Lucy. If something happened to her because of me—I'd never be able to live with myself. But, thank you for this morning, too. Taking me to the hospital. We only saw Catherine through a window, but we did see her, and she is alive and...they did let her sister sit by her and hold her hand. That was good to see."

He nodded. "Of course," he said quietly. "Okay, so—to the museum."

Soon, they were in the section that told the story of Micah Stratford, born outside of Springfield, Missouri, in 1838, married to Eliza Peacock in 1859. He'd started riding with friends in the years before the Civil War—until he saw what his friends were doing. The horror story of both sides committing cold blooded murder left him horrified, and he'd gone home to work his farm. Then was declared, and he'd joined a regular army unit.

After the war, he'd made his way west—like so many other men and women who had lost everything, or worse, those they had loved.

"This is the saddest story," Sienna murmured. "He left his rough-riding friends when he found out what they were doing—and, then, in the end, he was killed by them. He was just trying to do the right thing."

"The thing that made it a small note in the history of the area, is that those men he had once thought to be his friends were monsters—they weren't even really on a side—they just liked terrorizing farmers in Missouri and Kansas. When the war was over, they started up the same in the old west, torturing people, killing their livestock, vandalizing equipment—all to get their land, certain they would find a big haul. None of it was right—not when we pride ourselves as a nation on our sense of justice and mercy—but, because of that gunfight, people went on to live decent lives and the area was settled. I'm incredibly proud of him, of course."

"What about Eliza?" she asked him, smiling. She was looking at the display, and a picture of Eliza next to the original Micah Stratford.

"Eliza opened a school, one of the first people to insist that children of all colors and national origin were welcome. No one fought her—because Micah was dead, and they all had a chance at life because of Micah. She helped out neighbors—and she mourned for him the rest of her life while raising their children. To do what she did, she had to be a very strong woman, and, of course, a generous woman. Sometimes we turn our pain into depression and very bad things—sometimes, we turn it into something that can, at the least, help others."

"Well, she was very beautiful—and, the only thing we have in common is long dark-blond hair," Sienna said. "I don't look a thing like her."

He grinned. "And, in my case, decades of mixed genetics have meant that I don't look a hell of a lot like my ancestor. That's what I can't figure. You may be right; a ghost, memories of something that you've read triggered in your mind to help— something. Because, how the hell do you look that much like someone else?"

She stared at the wall and the pictures of the past.

"He is a ghost, and if everyone thinks I'm crazy, it's all right. So far, Catherine Maddox is alive."

"Thanks to you."

She shook her head. "No, you insisted we go at night—I would have suggested the morning. And she would have been dead by then."

"We make a good team," he said, offering her a dry grimace.

"Let's hope we can find whoever did this—and, I know how hard this is to believe, but, we won't find him dressed up as your ancestor." She hesitated. "I know how crazy this sounds, but, I think he's done what he needed to do."

He took her by the shoulders, looking into her eyes. "Sienna, I believe you."

"You believe in ghosts?"

"I believe in you."

She was looking up at him with such hope and such trust, hair tumbling around her shoulders, eyes such a crystal combo of green and gold. Her mouth was generous, her lips were tempting, and he fought the urge to simply lower his head and kiss her.

Not right; not now. He wouldn't take advantage of her vulnerable state of mind.

"Back to the conference," he said, clearing his throat, and he touched her elbow to lead her toward the exit.

A   killer   was   still   out   there.

Chapter 8

"What great timing!" Lucy said. She beamed as Sienna walked into the room where the video equipment was set up. "I have a chance to go to a late lunch with my favorite sci-fi author, ever! Oh, this is Melvin Hunter, from security," she said, introducing the man from security who had been sent to watch over the room—and Lucy. "He'll be staying with you all day."

Melvin Hunter had been sitting. He stood and welcomed Sienna with a handshake. "Nice to meet you," he said.

"A pleasure, and thank you," Sienna returned.

"Melvin has been great—during our off times, we've been looking at each other's baby pics on our phones. Melvin has a three-year-old little girl. She's adorable."

"Congratulations," Sienna told him.

He smiled.

"Well, let's talk shop," Lucy said, making a face that indicated that she wanted to speak with Sienna alone.

"I'll be right here, and I'll be with you—unless you're in a large-audience workshop, and if so, I'll be waiting right after," Melvin promised, pointing to a chair back behind the camera.

"Thank you!" Sienna told him.

Lucy pulled her aside, smiling.

She quickly lost her smile, though, worried as brought Sienna across the room to ask anxiously, "She's still alive, right? Catherine Maddox, she's still alive?"

"Yes, yes, she's in a coma, in intensive care, but, she's stable and the doctors feel that she'll be all right. Dehydration does all kinds of things to the body, and they're doing their best to make sure that her organs are recovering well, that they do plenty of brain scans...but, everyone is encouraged."

"Because of you!" Lucy said. "My best friend is a heroine!"

"Please, please, you didn't say anything, right? Captain Murdock was very careful to keep my name out of the paper, they said that she was found because of an anonymous tip. Lucy, you didn't say anything to anyone, right?"

Lucy made a little sign of the cross over her chest. "Thank God, she's alive, one way or the other, and no, I didn't say a word to anyone. How long have you known me? When have I ever broken a promise or a confidence?"

"Never," Sienna admitted.

Lucy grinned. "You may not like the reason I said that I was subbing for you!"

"And what was that?"

"I said that you were on a date, and that you'd gone out—leaving me most ably in charge, of course—because you had a date. And, of course, that was the truth. You did have a date—even if that date was to go to the hospital and check on the woman you'd saved."

Sienna let out a sigh. "I didn't save her—I really didn't. I thought that Micah should have called the cops and that they should have started looking in the morning. If it hadn't been for him..."

"Well, then, between you—pretty darned good partnership. Okay, I know you're going to be with Micah, but, keep texting me, whatever, so that I know you're all right."

"I will. I promise. And you keep up with me."

"I will. Oh, look, by the way—I wasn't kidding about the exchange of baby pictures. Look what hubby just sent me!"

Lucy whipped out her phone and keyed up her pictures. "Hubby just sent me a video—hang on, have to hit the right button.

She did. There was little Morgan, a beautiful little boy, at the New Orleans zoo, smiling and laughing in front of a habitat for monkeys. One of them was imitating Morgan. Morgan was imitating the monkeys, laughing. Then he looked at the camera and said—un-coaxed by his father—and said, "I love you, Mommy. I miss you. I wish you were here."

"He's so adorable—I forget I needed a bit of a break!" Lucy said.

"He is adorable—and you're the best mother ever," Sienna assured her. "Now, go—go meet your favorite sci-fi author. I have the reigning king of books for children on his way in. I'm happy I get to handle it. I love his work, and I've heard he's the nicest man in the world."

"I'm going—I'm on my way out!" Lucy said. "Keep in touch, promise?"

"You got it—and you keep in touch, too, promise."

Lucy crossed her heart and went out.

"I can help you with anything you need," Melvyn reminded her, looking up from the book he'd picked up to read himself.

He smiled at Sienna. "I grew up loving this guy's stuff—I can't believe I'll be here while you're interviewing him!"

"Well then, I'm awfully glad you will be."

"These books on the table...I mean, I don't want to take advantage here, but..."

"They're mine, picked up for the interviews. When it's over, I'm sure he'll sign it to you."

Melvyn looked at her with far more gratitude than she deserved. "Thank you!" he said, his voice husky. "For my little girl. I can help you, too, with anything tech." He smiled. "Good day all around—they found Miss Maddox, and now...I get to meet my childhood hero!"

"Did you know her?" Sienna asked.

"I saw her on the floor a few times. Always nice to everyone. I'm so grateful they found her. She tipped well, too, and didn't slam the machines or anything if she lost. I think anyone she saw had to have believed she was a really nice person. Amazing that they got to her just in the nick of time!"

Sienna attempted a smile.

Amazing. And all because of...

A ghost?

***

So much footage; so many cameras.

It was a casino.

Thankfully, Milt had Rory Paxton helping him again, and maneuvering through what seemed like miles and miles of video could be navigated. At first, he'd been looking at everything. Now, he needed to narrow down. He had only the one clue—the way the kidnapper, and probably killer, moved.

"I did get it all separated," Rory Paxton told him. "I have all the days that Catherine Maddox was here, and all the footage in which she appears. I have the hallways and the elevators, and, of course, followed her movements off the elevator every day. It will still take some time, but, I can fast forward, pause, you know—do whatever you need."

"Thanks, Rory," Micah said.

He'd spent so much time watching Catherine Maddox.

Now, he needed to spend his time watching others—others who worked at the casino.

The only thing he had to go on was the way that a man moved.

He watched video for an hour, following Catherine everywhere she went.

Then, he went over the footage in which he believed someone was in costume—as in, the giant maid he had seen.

The costume was clever—a regular uniform, but, a cap, a lot of dark hair pinned up—and then a dust mask. A lot of the help wore them; they protected against germs and dust, and were akin to wearing gloves when cleaning.

"I know this is him," Micah murmured.

"I think you're right," Rory said. "I mean...we are an equal opportunity employer, but, that is one...strange looking woman. If it is a woman. I mean, that has to be a man dressing up, right?"

"And, someone who knows the cameras," Micah said. "There's never a shot of the face, never a clear shot of the face."

"You're right—not in the elevator, and not in the hallway," Rory said.

"Date this, and pull up employee records—who was working that day? Find out what maid was assigned to the floor and the room," Micah said.

Rory immediately went to work, pushing buttons on his computer. He sat back, frowning at Micah.

"Rosemary Hidalgo."

"Did she call in sick or anything that day?"

Rory looked at his computer. "No."

"Okay, I know you separated all this, but bring up the rest of the afternoon in which we had our very strange maid in the hotel."

Rory did so. "Rosemary, yes. I know her. Nice older woman, working hard, just got her citizenship, and...there she is—look. It's a few hours later, and she's in the hall. There—she opens the door and comes out looking confused. Because the room has already been cleaned."

Micah leaned forward. The woman looked at her chart, and then back at the door—and then she shrugged.

The room had been cleaned. It was obvious she assumed she'd been given the room number in error—or, that the guest had stayed out through the night.

It happened at a casino.

"Okay, sorry—one more time, our fake maid."

Rory complied. Micah studied the movement of the person who had gone in to Catherine Maddox's room.

Who had gone in to handle her belongings, perhaps to lie on her sheets, and touch her in that far distance and frightening way.

It was, he thought, the same person who had pretended to be a nun, who had stopped Catherine Maddox on the street, who had left that frightened look in her eyes.

"Okay, sorry, Rory, now...back to Catherine moving through the hotel. I want to see which casino people might have taken a special interest in her."

"You think it's someone in the casino?"

"Could be."

Rory gave himself a shake.

"Because they know how to get in and out as a maid?"

"Inner knowledge of the workings—the entrances and exits and all—yes, that would be my reasoning."

He'd been a cop. He wanted to vet certain people first. He didn't bother with Milt; he'd known him forever. He didn't have the slightly awkward walk—barely noticeable—of their kidnapper. But, there were others in the hotel and casino he had long known and trusted.

He'd start there—right after he checked out Melvyn Hunter.

Just to be on the logically safe side.

***

Sienna's interview came and went—and her author had proven to be the incredibly nice man she'd always heard that he was.

Melvyn got his autographed book, and all had gone well.

Of course, they'd all talked about the woman who had disappeared—only to be found last night, in the nick of time.

Everyone would be talking about it that day.

It had happened here, in the area, all between Reno and Virginia City.

She was alive, so it wasn't just a topic of conversation, it was a topic of good conversation. Naturally, everyone wanted to know if the police had a suspect.

By five, Sienna had finished her interviews for the day. A marketing guru—supposedly one of the best to be had anywhere—was speaking at five. Of course, he'd be speaking about social media, newsletters, podcasts, video channels, and other venues that had come into being for authors to grow an audience. Lucy would be there, paying grave attention, and listening for anything marketing that might be good for her as far as turning works of art into pictures, postcards, or other saleable work.

Sienna knew she had risked everything, coming up with the capital to start the restaurant. Anything she learned might be helpful in that direction, too.

"Melvyn, want to walk me to the main hall? I'm going to go to the major workshop for the day—and don't worry. It will be me and about a thousand of my new best friends."

"I will be happy to escort you," he told her, "and I will wait for you by whichever door you enter—two to the right of the stage, and two to the left," he told her. "Just make sure you come back to the right place."

"I will—and I do know left from right, so we'll be fine. I think we're out of coffee in the room—I know Ernie set Lucy up this morning, but by this time, well, anyway, take the time and get something for yourself if you like."

"Oh, no. I'll be waiting. At the door, right where I leave you."

Sienna thanked him, and then headed down the hallway with several hundred people, all going to see the man who was speaking. Some were still working on projects they hadn't tried to self-pub or submit anywhere as yet, others were fledgling authors, and others, still, were popular—so popular that they were household names. They laughed and chatted together, and Sienna was impressed with the group—not a prima donna among them, no matter how popular a man or woman might be.

Melvyn hung right by her side as they walked, smiling as well when she waved or greeted people she knew.

When they reached the main conference room, Sienna looked around, hoping to find Lucy. She didn't see her friend anywhere, and the room was filling up quickly—she didn't really want to relegate herself to 'standing room only,' so she turned to Melvyn.

"Okay, going in."

He smiled at her. "I'll be right here."

Sienna found a seat among the authors pouring in, still looking for Lucy all the while. She frowned, thinking that her friend would definitely have come to this workshop—it was one of the program slots that Lucy hadn't just marked—she'd put a bunch of stars next to it on her program.

Of course, there were hundreds of people in the room. The conference itself—being in a casino town, taking in all forms of the written word and offering amazing special guest speakers—had garnered about three-thousand attendees. It was easy to understand that with the hundreds of people flooding the aisles and taking their chairs, she couldn't see her friends. Lucy wouldn't have been expecting her, either—she'd think that she was back either editing her footage and that she might have snagged another author.

Conversations flooded the room, then the conference host introduced their next speaker—and the audience went silent—people were hanging on every word.

It really was a great speech. The world had changed with the age of the Internet—publishing had changed, as they all knew. That didn't mean that all forms of publishing couldn't be completely valid, and it was up to each individual to learn how to create a career.

The point was though, that, in the way it had changed, whether an author was with a traditional house, a small house, or doing self-pub, it was incredibly important that they know about marketing and self-promotion. It was still the same game—people couldn't buy what they couldn't see.

For a while, Sienna listened attentively. But, even as she listened, she still tried to watch the room. No sign of Lucy.

She was just growing really worried when she saw that Lucy was calling her. Luckily, she had turned her ringer off, so the people sitting next to her weren't ready to drag her out.

She didn't answer the ring; she texted instead.

I'm in the marketing workshop. Where are you? I thought that you'd be in here.

There wasn't an answer at first; Lucy must have gotten distracted.

Sienna even started paying attention to the speaker again.

Then, she felt the vibration in her phone that told her she had a text.

I need you.

She quickly answered.

You need me where? What's going on?

Lucy answered within a few seconds.

I'm in trouble.

So much for the workshop.

You're in trouble where—what happened? What do you want me to do?

Once again, the answer came quickly.

Please, come out to your left—I need to talk to you now. Excuse yourself and come out now. I need you desperately. Please!

She looked to where she knew Melvyn was waiting for her but knew she couldn't ignore Lucy; there were hundreds of people by her. She couldn't possibly be in any danger.

Hating the fact that she was doing it, she crawled over people as quickly as she could, trying to disturb as few people as possible, and muttering inwardly about what she was going to do to Lucy if this didn't prove to be really important. What could her friend have done—skipped the workshop for a slot machine, gotten mad at the machine—and knocked it over?

It sure didn't sound as if she'd hit a jackpot.

Sienna escaped the conference room. There were a number of people milling around in the hall, engaged in conversations here and there. Melvyn wasn't there—he was waiting right where he was supposed to be waiting—on the other side.

She looked around and didn't see Lucy. She started to text again, to ask her friend where she was.

Her phone rang. Lucy.

Except it wasn't Lucy.

A man's voice spoke to her.

"Miss Johnston, listen to me, listen well, and don't move, don't drop your phone, don't make any sound. I have your friend, sweet, cheerful, giving, Lucy. You know, of course, that she has a loving husband and a precious child. She's in so much danger right now. But, you see, you're the one I want. So, this is all up to you. I'm watching, of course."

She gripped the phone tightly, hearing a muffled cry of distress in the background. Then, Lucy must have freed herself, because she was gasping and trying to shout loud enough to be heard over the cell phone.

"Don't, don't, Sienna, don't, he'll just kill the both of us. Run, get help, get—"

Lucy stopped speaking with a strangled cry.

Sienna felt her heart beat, heard it, as if it was a drumbeat in her ears. She was terrified; Lucy. Lucy, who was the mother of a toddler, a wife, a friend, one of the best human beings Sienna had ever known.

She couldn't be terrified; she needed to think. She couldn't act in panic—they would both die.

"I'll do what you want," she said. "But, I want Lucy first. I want to know that Lucy is all right—I need some kind of a guarantee."

"Get to the entrance," the voice commanded.

"I'll go to the entrance, but, I won't take another step until I know that Lucy is safe."

A soft laughter sounded, evil in its depth. "Well, you'll have to play it my way. I give you Lucy here, and you just run to the cops or your boy toy, Sienna." The 'S' in her name was sibilant, as if he was imitating a snake. "Go to the entrance; I'll call you again there."

The phone went dead.

Sienna looked back. The workshop was beginning to break up; people would be spilling out.

Melvyn would be looking for her.

She tried to see through the people. There was no sign of Melvyn, but there were so many people...

She hurried to the casino entrance before he could realize that she wasn't there.

And that she wouldn't be coming out, grateful that she couldn't see him...

Which meant, most likely, that he couldn't see her.

***

Melvyn was the poster boy for what a woman would look for in man. Graduated high school at the top of his class, joined the armed forces, did his time, and used his military college benefits to major in business. He was going to grad school and working part time at the casino while he finished his schooling.

But, it wasn't his stellar record that made Micah hesitate; he'd never seen the man favor one leg over the other, and Milt had sworn by him.

He had, however, received a serious injury to his right leg in the Middle East.

He watched video of the man on duty. He didn't see any form of limp.

He moved on.

He'd known Milt his whole life; he still watched video of his friend coming and going.

He looked at the entire security force and saw nothing unusual. He thought back to the morning when he had first come over at Milt's invitation—and seen Sienna Johnston for the first time.

He'd spoken with Gary Morgan, one of the floor managers that morning, and Ernie Anderson, at the coffee bar. He turned to Rory.

He stared back at the screen. He'd been through the security force over, and over.

He'd been through the housekeepers, the floor managers, even the dealers and the slot attendants.

Now, it was time to go through outside vendors, restaurant employees, and anyone at all who worked within the hotel/casino walls.

Melvyn's picture was still on the screen, but, his thoughts had moved on.

He stood abruptly.

"I've got to find Sienna," he told Rory, and he was already out of the security room, heading to the conference room, and dialing Artie as he did so.

Chapter 9

Maybe Melvyn had seen me come through—maybe he will follow me, unbeknownst to whoever was holding Lucy. Maybe he will stop me.

She didn't want him to stop her. Anything happening to Lucy—when she had a husband and her little boy—was debilitating. She couldn't bear the thought that she had caused her friend's trauma now, and that she might cause her death.

The phone rang again. It was Lucy's number calling; it was her attacker on the phone.

"You're outside; good girl. Good girl. Hop a cab to Beulah's—it's a restaurant not far from you, in another casino. Wait there. I'll be by, white van. If there is anyone near you—and, trust me, I know the security—I will obviously be caught. But, your friend Lucy will die. I will shoot her before I'm shot down myself, do you understand?"

"I understand," she said numbly.

She walked up to the valet who asked her if she was all right before she said that she needed a cab. She assured him that she was fine, although she was so frozen she didn't know what she was doing.

He knows he'll get caught; he doesn't care. He will die, but he will make Lucy die, too. I will most probably die if I go to him, but he has Lucy...

It was only about five minutes to the other casino and the fronting restaurant. Still feeling ice cold and certain that she had become a robot, Sienna got out. She stood at the entrance along with others waiting for their cars, or cabs, or just to be picked up.

There can't be any security with her, but he didn't say anything about my phone. She texted frantically, Micah's number. *White van, a male, taking me from Beulah's...help. I'm so sorry—he has Lucy.*

She saw the white van and eased her phone back into her purse.

She didn't move toward it; she waited.

Her phone rang. She dug it back out.

"What are you doing?" the voice—on Lucy's line—demanded.

"I'm not getting in until Lucy gets out," Sienna told him.

"Come to the van; I'll let her out as I let you in.

The van was on the far side of the massive driveway with all its blinking neon.

"I will not get in until I see her out," she said harshly.

"Fine. But, get closer. Oh, she isn't dead—I swear it. She's a little stoned. But, you keep your side of the bargain, I'll keep mine. She can get out on her own, and I'm sure someone will help her. If you don't get over here in two minutes, though, I'll drop her out—dead. Oh, and you will get in the van after you see her—or I'll shoot her then. Do you understand? I will do it."

Sienna watched for the cars and cabs sliding through the entrance and walked carefully to the other side. She kept a distance from the van. The side door opened; Lucy came out.

She saw him, glancing back at her from the driver's seat.

Him...

So hard to tell; he was wearing a prosthetic. His forehead and nose were too large, his chin too small. He looked like...

A cartoon character.

Lucy stumbled from the van, looking like a zombie; Sienna started to reach for her.

"No!" the driver ordered, and she heard a click as he discretely aimed his gun at Lucy's back.

She stumbled by Sienna; a valet racing to help her.

"Get in. Or, I can shoot you now. You're thinking, you clever girl. You may die, but, you'll bring me with you. But! Get in the van—you can live a while longer on hope."

Hope apparently did spring eternal in the human heart. She got in the van.

Even as she crawled in, she realized, incredulously, just who her attacker was.

***

Micah raced down to Sienna's video room; it was empty, calling Artie as he did so, and telling him what he thought to be the truth.

Dozens of people were coming out of the main conference room; he made his way through them, thinking—praying—that she might still be there, chatting with authors, marketers, or others who had attended.

He went through dozens of people; he couldn't find her—or Lucy. Maybe she and Lucy had both attended. Maybe they were doing business—what they had come to Reno to do.

Where the hell is Melvyn?

He made his way through a dozen more groups, people standing around in small groups, all excited, all happy about the speech they had just listened to.

At last, he saw Melvyn.

But, seeing Melvyn was no assurance; the man looked as desperate as he felt.

"Where is she? What happened?"

"I don't know—I did everything that Milt told me to do. I didn't let her go to the ladies' room without walking her down the hall. He said she was all right in a big crowd; I stayed at the door. She knew right where I was, and that she was going to come back to me when it was over. There were so many people. I watched, I—I know how to watch someone. No one threatened her. People got up, I caught one woman who had been next to her, and she said she snuck out right before it was over—and went to the other doors. I made my way here..."

Micah felt his phone buzzing. He looked at and almost took a breath of relief.

Sienna.

But then it seemed that his blood congealed.

He read her text, hung up at the last word, and dialed Artie. "He has her. I know I'm right, and it's him. He kidnapped Lucy and used threats against her to get Sienna. He picked her up in front of Beulah's in white van."

"I've already got an all-points bulletin out on him," Artie said. "I can meet you at Beulah's. Does he have her—or does he have her and Lucy. Wait!"

Artie paused a minute and got back on the phone. "We've just had a call in—Lucy is alive, and a mess. Paramedics picked her up—from in front of the restaurant. She's being rushed to the hospital. Maybe, just maybe, she can tell us something."

"On my way. Artie, you've got to talk to Murdock. We have to get men out in force. He may leave her with oxygen—like he did Catherine Maddox. Or he may not. We have to find him before he buries her. Or dumps her. Or—"

"Micah, we'll find her. The whole force will be out," Artie promised.

Micah knew he had to get it together. He turned to Melvyn. "Anything—you hear anything at all that might help, you call me."

"I'll get a search going in the casino—"

"She's not in the casino. But, if you hear anything, call me."

He didn't want to take the time to explain to Melvyn. He hurried out to the valet. "Hey," one of the men he knew called. "Your friend just left, the pretty, pretty blond. She was...off. I just thought I should tell you—"

"I need my car. Fast. Please."

"On it. She looked off, but she left of her own volition."

"Your car is coming now."

"Thanks!"

His car rolled up; he almost jerked the valet driving out of it.

Ten minutes brought him to the hospital, and another two brought him into emergency where Lucy was still being treated. She was sobbing, tears running down her cheeks.

"Go easy; she's better now. We're still trying to get his mix of sedatives out of her system. I'm not sure it's been a good idea—she's so upset. Said a friend took her place with a monster. The guy who got Catherine Maddox, I take it," the doctor told him.

He hurried to Lucy's side, kneeling down by her. She clutched his hand, sobbing, her grip so strong he had to take care that she didn't knot her IV.

Lucy started speaking, hysterically.

"He has her...he's a monster. He got me and kept me in the van. I was so stupid. When he said that he needed my help, I fell for it...I walked right out. He has a gun and a knife, and he didn't care about me, didn't care about me at all...he just wanted Sienna. I didn't believe it...I couldn't believe that he wanted her so badly. I didn't let him call...he got my phone. She came to him insisting that he let me go. She made him let me out of the car...he had the gun. I could barely stand. She did it because he said he didn't care—if she brought help, he'd die, but he'd make sure that he killed me first. Micah, you have to find her, you have to find her..."

"Yes, I need your help. Where did he take you? What did he say—can you remember anything?"

She shook her head. "All I know is the van, but..." She paused, frowning. "I don't know what he gave me...I'm trying so hard to remember. He muttered a lot. He hates you. Says you...says he was going along all right. But, you were going to ruin everything. He's watched you. He knew that you were called in."

"Of course, he does," Micah said bitterly.

"He...he was talking about you, about the museum, about your ancestor...he was muttering that you think you're him, wanting to take down the bad guys."

He looked up; Artie had arrived.

"We're stopping every white van in the city; we'll find her," he said.

Micah stood. "Look for white vans—I'm heading to my place. He's going to try to kill her, and, I believe, he's going to do it on my property."

"You own hundreds of acres." Artie said.

"Lucy, if anything else...Artie will leave a man here with you, okay. If you think of anything else, have him call me right away."

He hesitated, standing straight, and looking at Artie.

"Have your men watch and report white vans; don't let them approach. If they try to apprehend him, he'll kill her. I'm heading out. I think we'll need a search party at my place."

Artie nodded, pulling out his phone.

Lucy was sobbing again. Micah took a minute to lean down by her again. "Lucy, I'm going to get him. I promise you, I'm going to get him."

"I still don't even know who he is. He had stuff on his face, like a nose and a forehead. I don't even know who he is, what he looks like."

"I do," Micah told her grimly.

***

Sienna had seen him every morning since she'd come to the hotel. She'd felt badly for the way people treated him.

She'd been nice to him.

She stared at him as he drove; he had her in the passenger seat while he drove with one hand—keeping his gun aimed at her with the other.

He smiled suddenly. "You're thinking, what the hell? Why is this guy after me? I'm nice when I order my coffee. I leave a nice tip. Yep, sure, that's you. Little Miss Sunshine. Just like that Catherine Maddox."

She wasn't sure how she managed to speak, but, she did. And she did so sounding absurdly calm.

"Yes, well, we were both raised to be courteous, I imagine," she said.

"And that's just it. You think that you're courteous—and because of that, you're all high and mighty. But, my dear Miss Johnston, it's lip service. It's all lip service. I saw you that first morning you were in the hotel—being nice, but looking right past me, right through me. You didn't see me—you were looking beyond me. You were looking at Mr. Cool—Mr. Hot-Shot, not a cop any longer, but, hell, called by every cop in the damned region when there's a problem. He couldn't cut it, you know. You were a fool, looking at him—and looking right past me."

"Did that really matter? You like killing women. You like murdering them."

He smiled at that. "I give them a chance. In different ways, I give them a chance. That last one, you even saved her ass. Just in time. How the hell you did that, I don't know. I'm going to give you a chance, too. Give Hot-Shot a chance to save you. You get oxygen, too."

"How kind."

"It is a kindness."

"Of course, they'll know who you are now."

"You think—your friend had no clue." He smiled. "I was a performer, you know. I had a comedy act, and then a juggling act—and then some bimbo told me that I wasn't getting jobs because I was too ugly. I let her see ugly," he said softly. "And then, I learned to make ugly work."

I should just try to jump out of the car.

If she did, she would die.

I could save others from this fate.

But, it was still there. Hope.

Instead of hope, she wished she'd had classes in self-defense or fire-arms. She had no idea what the gun he carried was, or what kind of ammunition he used.

Lethal, she imagined.

She looked out the window and realized that they were heading for Micah's property. There was at least a mile before the museum and the ranch house that was little but trees and scruff and brush—and trails through them. Just as she thought that he could take her into what was ostensibly wilderness, he jerked off the road, and onto a bumpy trail.

His truck bounced and rolled over the rough terrain, but he managed to keep the wheel and his grip on the gun.

She wasn't sure where he was going, when he suddenly jerked to a halt behind a large group of trees and shrubs.

"Out," he told her.

The gun remained aimed at her. She could run...

"Don't do it—I don't want to give you the mix I gave your friend. Not sure about her...think she'll be okay, but, hey...what, do I look like a druggist? Then again, maybe you'll live longer if you're not frantically trying to breathe."

She crawled out; he crawled out behind her.

He had a tank—just like the one that had been with Catherine Maddox—ready for her. He didn't even look at it as he reached for it.

He gave her a macabre smile—made so by the prosthetics on his face. Or made so by whatever demons tore his mind apart.

"Walk," he said.

"Walk where?"

"Ahead of me, that way. You'll know when to stop."

She took several steps and then paused, stunned.

He was in front of her—her ghost. The cowboy who had first appeared to her in a video game, and who had then approached her at the museum, and in the cemetery...

Micah Stratford. The original Micah Stratford.

Her heart began to beat. But, he was dead. He couldn't help her. He couldn't do anything to Ernie Anderson.

Ernie couldn't even see him.

"Eliza!" the ghost cried, his tone broken and agonized.

"Keep walking!"

She moved forward. The ghost fell into step with her. "Eliza, I have to find a way...Micah, I have to get to him, I have to..."

He disappeared. She kept walking.

She stopped again; he had told her that she would know when.

And she did. They had come upon one of his cheap pine boxes.

And a deep hole within the ground.

She turned back.

Ernie Anderson, the harried coffee shop clerk—harboring a deep-seated resentment against women who were polite, but, in his mind, never saw him--was smiling at her again.

That macabre smile.

"Be a good girl and get in—that is, be a good girl if you want the oxygen. It will buy you many hours that you might not have had, as you know, of course."

She smiled back. "I'd have never gone out with you—if I'd really seen you, I guarantee, I'd have never gone out with you. I wouldn't have even been your friend."

She crawled into the box.

Chapter 10

Micah drove to the museum, barely turned the truck off before jumping out, and heading for the stables. The only way to really make his way through the property was on horseback.

He didn't bother with a saddle, but quickly bridled Stan, his favorite chestnut, a thoroughbred he'd rescued and a horse familiar with the terrain.

Heading back along the trail, he saw that Artie was true to his word—police cars were heading down the road toward the museum.

He reined in Stan and rode up to Artie's car.

"Is there a van on the property?" Artie asked.

"No, but, it's here—somewhere. Any of your men who can ride...they can find help in the museum. Get them mounted up so they can take the trails. There are rough roads that will accommodate vehicles, but, wherever he is—he isn't in the van anymore. He's going to bury her, Artie. We have to find out where."

"Checked the stats you gave me—Ernie Anderson did travel around to all those places. Tech pulled credit cards, judge gave an instant order...he is our man. We will get him, Micah."

Micah nodded grimly. They'd get him—but, even if they caught him on the road right now, he'd never say where he had taken Sienna.

He had to either find Sienna—or get to the man first. He was damned glad that he wasn't a cop at the moment.

He didn't notice the tire tracks at first; the roads were so dry and pebble-strewn that little was showing. But, as the cop cars sped by him, he saw that a vehicle had turned off into the woods and scruff. He walked Stan along, searching again. The sun was going down and the light was fading.

He dismounted, walking Stan along with him, bent over, searching the rugged terrain.

It was then that he saw him. At first, a trick of the light.

Or a trick in his mind.

He blinked. Blinked against the dying sunset and the mauves that seemed to cover the world.

He was still there, beckoning to him.

He mounted Stan again, loping toward the apparition.

It didn't disappear.

When he reached the ghost, it still didn't disappear. "Time to get the bad guy, son, time to get the bad guy," he said.

His voice was the breeze; the rustle of the air.

But Micah heard it.

"She's not Eliza," the ghost said. "She's not my Eliza. But, she is yours, and there isn't much time. Hurry now."

Micah didn't question his mind or his sense anymore.

He followed.

***

"Let me be nice," Ernie Anderson said. "The tubes fit over you so...and, you're such a good girl, I'll leave the nozzle right where you can reach it. Now, I wouldn't try to use it yet—you'll have some air in the box and you'll need it. So, don't panic and turn that nozzle too fast!"

Sienna didn't reply. She was shaking so badly she could barely crawl into the box.

I should just rush him, let him shoot me!

But, they were on Micah's property. He could...he could find her. He really could.

She lay down in the pine box. Of all the things she had imagined happening to her in her life, being buried alive had never been one of them.

She lay still, arms by her side.

"What a good girl—what a nice girl," he said. "There—there's your oxygen. And now..."

The lid came over her.

Everything was darkness.

Then, everything was pain as he dragged the box to the giant hole in the earth, and she fell, with the box, down several feet into the earth.

She heard the sound as dirt was shoveled on top of the box, tasted the dust that came through the pine, and covered her.

***

Micah rode hard, following the ghost. He reined in as they came to the van, behind trees and shrubs, hidden far from the main road.

"Hurry!"

To his amazement, he heard the word as if it had been a shout.

"On foot," the ghost commanded.

Micah dismounted instantly. The ghost was moving ahead of him, fast in the coming darkness. Micah followed him.

He thrashed through trees and scrub, and then paused, gasping for breath, determined that he had to be quiet, lest there be an ambush planned for him.

And then he dead stopped by a tree. He could see Ernie Anderson.

The man's face was completely converted with the prosthetics he was wearing, and he looked like a maddened Elephant Man. He was shoveling dirt back into a big hole in a small clearing in the dense trees and foliage.

He hadn't seen Micah yet.

Micah wanted to shoot him; shoot him with no warning, with no...

Shoot to kill.

"No," the ghost said softly. "No."

The ghost of his ancestor moved into the clearing, doing his best to stir up dust and dirt and managing to divert the man's attention.

It worked. Ernie paused, frowning, looking in the other direction. And in that moment, Micah went after him, tackling him down with a fury born of fear and pent up anger against all those who would prey upon others.

They fell in the dirt together, and Micah had him with one good right to the jaw. He dragged him to his feet, turned him around, and ripped off his belt, creating a makeshift form of handcuffs. Then he threw him back to the earth, aimed his Colt at him, and warned, "One move. One move, and you're a dead man—except I'll kick the shit out of you first, hurt you really badly, maybe blow up a kneecap, you hear me?"

"You can't, you can't—that's not legal!" Ernie spat out.

"No? I'm not a cop, so...well, I don't really care. I'm an enraged citizen. Trust me—I'll get away with it."

He wanted to dig; dig instantly and madly. But, he forced himself to call Artie first.

Then, he took the man's shovel, and he began to dig, one eye on Ernie while he did so.

He had just reached the box when Artie and his men made their way through the trail.

Two of them rushed over to help him get the box out of the ground. Another had a crowbar.

And then...

The box was opened, and Sienna was staring up at him, shaking, but breathing easily, her arms outstretched. He pulled her into his own and held her. He knew that she was the most precious thing in the world to him.

The ghost had been right.

She wasn't Eliza, but she was his Eliza. Her named happened to be Sienna.

Epilogue

The night was long.

There was time spent at the police station, and then time spent at the hospital.

Thankfully, by the time they arrived, Lucy was doing well. They were going to release her the following morning.

She sobbed again, seeing that Sienna was safe. The two hugged for a very long time.

It was well past midnight—not really late by Reno standards—by the time they headed back to his ranch house. Sienna was desperate for a shower, and he showed her where everything was, then headed out.

He knew how he felt; he couldn't expect someone he'd met just days ago to feel the same. For some reason, he was ridiculously awkward, once it was over, once they had him, once they knew that Ernie Anderson was locked up, and would never leave a cell again.

But, Sienna walked out of the shower before starting, and asked, "You're not coming in with me?"

He rose, feeling almost as if he'd gone back to high school—he wasn't shy, in fact he was typically fairly confident, but...

She is my Eliza. That person I am meant to love...through life and death.

He tried to be logical and cool. "Listen, this has been a horrible night for you. You had to believe you were going to die several times. I took you out of the ground. You don't have to sleep with me because...I don't know. I'm sure a psychologist would have a term for what you have to be feeling, thinking that I saved you."

She smiled at that, those eyes of hers like the sweet fire.

"Okay, let's be honest here. You were spectacular; I believed you could save me—and you did. But, the first time I saw you, I thought you were infinitely fascinating. I think I had a few erotic dreams about you. Frankly, I'm sure Lucy was deeply disappointed that I didn't throw caution to the wind and sleep with you immediately. So...unless you just really don't want to join me, I'd love it if you would."

So, he did.

The shower washed away so much. Pain and fear, the demons that had plagued him. Her skin was silk, her kiss deep, and the passion between them as hot as the steaking water. Of course, he was way too big for shower sex, and kissing her and holding her, the two of them still dripping wet, he half-lifted her, and half carried her to the bed, where they fell down together, lips covering one another, hands everywhere, as frantic and urgent as it was possible to be.

She had a way with her...

Fingertips upon him, lips upon him, teasing and caressing his flesh.

He touched her, too, so needy, so desperate to know her, intimately and completely.

They made love and made love again.

And then again, and finally, exhausted and spent, they slept in one another's arms.

But, just before they did, he whispered softly to her.

"I didn't save you...well, I did save you. But, I couldn't have saved you—without him."

She turned into his arms, incredulous. "You saw him?" she asked on a breath.

He nodded solemnly. "I saw him, and he led me to you."

She curled against his side. "But, I'm not his Eliza, and he must know..."

"He does. You're not his Eliza. You're my Eliza."

The next morning, she wanted to stay out at the ranch. She would do other conferences, and she would open her restaurant, but she was all over the news and she simply didn't want to deal with others that day. It was too raw, too fresh, and when Lucy was out, she could gather all the attention, which she certainly deserved.

She wanted to head to the museum, and they did. They stood in front of the wall that held the photographs and the history of his family.

"I'm still so puzzled," she murmured. "When he talked to me, our ghost Micah first really seemed to think that I was his Eliza. And, I seriously don't look a thing like her."

Micah thought about her words, and then said, "Here is the only idea I can really grasp with that. We see differently when we're dead. We see people—and not the package of flesh and blood and bone. People talk about inner beauty, but, I believe from all this, that Micah saw Eliza in you—because of your heart, soul, kindness...all the things that do make up inner beauty. I mean, that's what I believe. I like to think, he saw himself in me. He knew that...that we could be together, could see the world with the same eyes, want good things...I don't know. I'm babbling, I believe. Grateful," he added softly.

"What a beautiful thought," she murmured. "You know, Ernie said that he took me because I was nice—but, didn't really see him."

"Don't let anything he said get to you!" Micah said angrily. "The man is sick. Your manner with people is beautiful."

"But, I don't want to see through anyone, which makes me think about Micah—our ghost Micah. I wish we could do something for him."

"I do, too. Flowers to the cemetery doesn't seem to fit the bill."

"But, let's bring some anyway."

They did.

It was nearly dusk when they came to the cemetery and the terrace where Micah's family plot was located. The colors of the dying day fell gently over old crosses, monuments, and tombstones, shading them in crimson, orange, and purple.

Sienna placed the flowers and stood back. As she did so, she gasped suddenly, pointing to a rise in the distance.

"Am I seeing things?" she asked in a whisper.

If she was, he shared her vision.

There, on that distant rise, was Micah. And walking toward him was a woman, dressed in a long gown, her hair flowing around her shoulders.

She stepped into his arms.

He held her, and then he turned to look back. Lifting an arm, he waved.

Then, the light fell, and they disappeared into the night.

"Will we see them again?" Sienna murmured.

He slipped his arms around and pulled her against him, still staring at that ridge where they had stood.

"I don't think so," he said. "They have each other. And, they know that we have each other. And that..."

She finished the thought for him.

"What we have will last a lifetime. And beyond."

And he knew it was true.

"Thank you," he said softly to the air.

"What will we do, though?"

"Time to get the bad guys," he told her.

"What?"

"I have to think it over, but, I have friends with the FBI in New Orleans. Maybe...or, maybe a cop again. I don't know."

"You'd give up the museum?"

"Never! But, I do have great people to run it, and I'm really good at buying airline tickets, so, I think we'd be fine."

"Two homes!" she said.

"One home. In your arms. Ouch, that was bad, that was..."

"I love it!" she assured him. "And you—through our lifetimes, and beyond."

New York Times and USA Today best-selling author Heather Graham majored in theater arts at the University of South Florida. After a stint of several years in dinner theater, back-up vocals, and bartending, she stayed home after the birth of her third child and began to write, working on short horror stories and romances. After some trial and error, she sold her first book, WHEN NEXT WE LOVE, in 1982 and since then, she has written over two hundred novels and novellas including category, romantic suspense, historical romance, vampire fiction, time travel, occult, and Christmas holiday fare. She wrote the launch books for the Dell's Ecstasy Supreme line, Silhouette's Shadows, and for Harlequin's mainstream fiction imprint, Mira Books.

Heather was a founding member of the Florida Romance Writers chapter of RWA and, since 1999, has hosted the Romantic Times Vampire Ball, with all revenues going directly to children's charity. She is pleased to have been published in approximately twenty languages, and to have been honored with awards from Waldenbooks. B. Dalton, Georgia Romance Writers, Affaire de Coeur, Romantic Times, and more. She has had books selected for the Doubleday Book Club and the Literary Guild, and has been quoted, interviewed, or featured in such publications as The Nation, Redbook, People, and USA Today and appeared on many newscasts including local television and Entertainment Tonight.

Heather loves travel and anything having to do with the water, and is a certified scuba diver. Married since high school graduation, and the mother of five, her greatest love in life remains her family, but she also believes her career has been an incredible gift, and she is grateful every day to be doing something that she loves so very much for a living.

Made in the USA
Coppell, TX
12 June 2020